RETURN

THE LAZARUS ALLIANCE: BOOK TWO

BLAZE WARD

KNOTTED ROAD PRESS

The Story Road

The Science Officer Series Season One
The Science Officer
The Mind Field
The Gilded Cage
The Pleasure Dome
The Doomsday Vault
The Last Flagship
The Hammerfield Gambit
The Hammerfield Payoff
The Bryce Connection

The Science Officer Series Season Two
Alien Seas

The Handsome Rob Gigs
Can't Shoot Straight Gang
Can't Shoot Straight Gang Returns
Hunting Handsome Rob
Handsome Rob, Assassin

Shadow of the Dominion
Longshot Hypothesis
Hard Bargain
Outermost
Dominion-427
Phoenix
Princess Rualoh

ONE

LAZARUS

IT FELT good to Lazarus to stride the decks of his warship *Ajax* again. He took a deep breath of the clean air and let it fill the depth of his lungs.

The atmosphere aboard the cargo runner *Shiva Zephyr Glaive* had always made him feel like he was standing at the top of a mountain, trying to breathe air too thin. Similarly, the gravity over there was only about eighty-five percent of what he had kept *Ajax* at when he commanded the ship.

He had finally come home.

And then been polite to his friends and turned the gravity down some. He supposed he could live at eighty-five percent for now. Similarly, he had backed off the atmospheric pressure a few notches, so that his friends wouldn't be unduly burdened by heavy air.

Some days, Lazarus felt like a Hun, or a space orc maybe, invading the prettier lands filled with sophisticated people unprepared for the strength, endurance, or potential for brutality that an average Human brought to the field.

He looked around the bridge of *Ajax* now as he entered. Friendly walls painted a soothing honey oak color a little softer than faded mustard, with the deck a dark gray that wouldn't show off the inevitable scuffs. Crew stations around him looked as pristine as the day they had launched, rather than fire-scorched and blood-splattered in the aftermath of near-destruction.

Thank God for the repair robots.

He and the others had been able to make most of the adjustments the ship had needed from an engineering console in the landing bay, after he had confirmed that the ship was steadily repairing itself, and that both cargo shuttles —that pair of specialized pinckes—were fully operational and ready to start hauling things back and forth.

Then they had spent the better part of four days moving things over, all the way down to draining the water tanks, so that *Shiva Zephyr Glaive* could be largely shut down and left in the same orbit that *Ajax* would be departing from.

Today had been his first real chance to walk all the way forward from cargo storage and the landing bay, into the command quarters area of the ship, and step onto what had been his bridge.

Before.

His mind still flashed back angrily to the moment he had dropped out of a test jump on the new star drives and landed right in the kill zone of a Westphalian GunWall. A full one, too. Twenty-one enemy warships. Sixteen Phalanxes, protecting four Archers, with that dreaded CommandWall vessel at the rear in command. *Ajax* could have taken on a simple Patrol, a Four and One, and pounded it into scrap, even with a new crew just learning their jobs. But a full GunWall had been too much, and he had been fighting for his life almost from the moment his blueshift had cleared.

"Thoughts?" a voice intruded. "You seem apprehensive or perhaps angry."

Lazarus turned to the man who had been his

commander, back over on the cargo runner. Director was the term these folks used, rather than Captain.

And *man* was only loosely accurate, if you wanted to get scientific.

Addison Wolcott. A Churquen, that is to say a naga-looking creature, all snake from the waist down and a scaled humanoid with spindly arms above that, but everyone in Innruld Space had spindly arms, compared to Humans. Only a Kreeghal had similar shoulders, and they sacrificed long legs for stubby ones barely capable of running. Addison had green and blue linear stripes, like the galaxy's largest garter snake.

The man's hazel eyes, slit vertically, missed little.

The other Churquen had joined Addison, the two of them still holding hands like giddy teenagers, if the occasional giggle that emerged was any cue.

Eha Dunham. Until recently, the woman had been a spymaster in charge of the cell of rebels that Addison represented. Unlike Addison, her scales were bright emerald, interrupted with linear stripes the color of honey. Her eyes were that same honey-amber color. They also barely missed anything, but she hadn't known Lazarus as long as the man who had rescued him originally.

After accidentally blowing up his shuttle, *Ajax*'s koch.

Well, Wybert had done that. The Ilount strove to be a warrior, worthy to eventually mate with his queen, but everyone else on the crew understood the term when Lazarus had suggested Wybert was a little soft in the head.

Aggressive and well-meaning. Loyal to a fault. About as safe as a six-year-old holding a loaded pistol.

At least the Ilount looked impressively martial. The body reminded Lazarus of a centaur as Wybert entered the bridge and clacked to a halt on ten, noisy feet. The man's bluish torso had four arms, upper pair and lower, and he was carrying his powerspear like that six-year-old who took his favorite teddy bear everywhere.

The five eyes, two large and three small, saw an impressive range of details. Two antennae, located on the sides of his head like horns, picked up scent and sound simultaneously.

Nobody could get Wybert not to wear his armor on the ship, any ship, so he had it on today: blue thorax covered by something like a light breastplate in a nicer shade, a turquoise, with the top side of his horizontal abdomen also armored over his natural scales from the waist all the way to his aft, where a pair of spinnerets emerged.

Four mandibles with big, ripping teeth feeding into a toothy maw was the stuff of nightmares as well, but Lazarus knew that Wybert mostly ate a thin gruel that tasted remarkably like honeyed oatmeal.

"What?" Wybert asked defensively as he realized Lazarus was looking at him.

"Welcome to your new home, Wybert," Lazarus said. "All the weapons systems are controlled from here, so we'll need to replace most of the furniture with something more comfortable."

"And I get to fire the guns?" he asked hopefully.

Six-year-old. In a candy-shop. With money from grandpa. Not that Lazarus had any such memories himself.

"You will," Lazarus assured him.

Wybert clattered happily off in the direction of the bridge.

"You're ignoring me," Addison said quietly.

"Trying to think of a polite way to answer you," Lazarus deflected him instead. "You asked if I was apprehensive or angry. Both, I think."

"So you don't think it was an accident that saw you and

Ajax nearly destroyed," Addison said, not particularly trying to make it sound like a question.

"The odds of that are about as good as landing in the middle of the Phraettis Nebula safely from a blind jump out of the Rio Alliance side," Lazarus chuckled, referring to the place where he had originated, where that grand nebula looked like a shield across a wide swath of the stars.

Lazarus had managed exactly that random feat of navigation, escaping that first battle, but it wasn't luck he wanted to try to recreate.

"And you still think it wise to return to your homeland?" Addison replied. "With, I might remind you, an entirely alien crew."

"Watch who you're calling alien, Scaly," a different voice intruded.

Kuei Akeley. Addison's pilot, back on the other ship. Smiling as wide as she could as she followed Wybert onto the spacious bridge.

The woman was a Vaadwig. To Lazarus, she always looked like an Australian kangaroo with a wider skull. The same heavy legs and big tail that almost made her look like a tripod. Fine sandy-brown fur covered her body where she wasn't also wearing her usual baggy leotard with the big pouch across the center. Armless and legless, it was still clothing, marking her as intelligent.

Just in case the sarcastic mouth ever failed to alert you.

Lazarus smiled at her as she waddled close.

"Where'm I going?" she asked, eyes almost as big and demonstrative as Wybert's, with just as much excitement.

Lazarus broke away from the two Churquen with a nod and guided his favorite Vaadwig to the station where his first star pilot had died. He wasn't superstitious, and the various robots and cleaning systems had left it spotless, but his mind could still place the splatters and pools of blood, both on the seat as well as dripping onto the metal deck.

"You'll be here, once we change seats for something you'll find comfortable," Lazarus smiled at her.

None of the bridge systems were turned on right now, so nothing bad happened as the woman leaned over and began memorizing keys and screens with her fingertips.

Muscle memory for later.

They were all here, even the crew who would rarely have a need to physically visit the bridge.

Ereshkiki Nisab, the Qooph wheelman who would eventually become something of a Chief Engineer, even if his preferred title was Systems Mechanic. Assuming that the Rio Alliance allowed Lazarus to keep his crew intact. There was always that risk, returning with a whole new set of species nobody there had ever even heard of.

Thadrakho the Necherle stayed close to Ereshkiki Nisab. A seven-foot-tall, skinny, off-white ice demon from somebody's worst nightmares; the armored, insectile creature was a fantastic mechanic with a powerful redneck streak. Always damned useful on any starship, let alone an experimental warship.

Khyaa'sha Ramarkhay, the species properly named a Tarni even though everyone called them pinwheel spiders, stayed near the door. On *Shiva Zephyr Glaive*, she had simply been the cook, if anything involving so many species could be considered simple. *Ajax* was largely automated, but someone needed to be in charge of the wardroom, and there was a full kitchen if you wanted to make it personal.

He could see her doing that. Hopefully, the food stores he had originally laid in for his shakedown cruise would prove palatable to the others. And not poisonous.

Cormac the NavCrawler was nearby, mostly staying as much out of the way as Khyaa'sha was. They hadn't had a chance to build any interfaces that would let a two-foot-by-two-foot-by-foot-tall sentient rolling computer communicate with *Ajax*.

Yet.

Well, there was an audio input channel, but the ship was designed for organics, *Humans*, to control everything. Even if Cormac had eleven decades of uptime at present.

"So, finally decided to quit?" Aileen asked as she stepped around Cormac's shell.

Aileen Enjehn. Yithadreph. Four and a half feet tall, a space otter covered over with dark brown fur. Today, her mobile whiskers were straight out sideways with humor that reached even to her eyes. She wore her favorite pearl-colored capri pants and banana-colored vest for the occasion.

"Might have gotten a better offer," Lazarus smiled back at her.

Down at her. He was a shade over six feet, and only Thadrakho was taller.

"I'm still going to be expecting you to be down in cargo occasionally, busting your ass to pack and unpack stuff," she volleyed with a laugh. "It'll keep you grounded and not too lazy."

"I'll see what I can do," Lazarus laughed.

It felt good to be able to laugh, especially with his new friends.

Five months ago, he had been a *Capitão De Mar E Guerra* with the Rio Alliance. Captain of Sea and War. Taking this very ship, this experimental wonder, on her shakedown cruise to make sure everything worked the way he had originally designed it.

Now he was something of a pirate in Innruld space, fleeing from the so-called Overlords of the Galaxy.

Lazarus was genuinely looking forward to one of these days introducing the Innruld specists to Westphalian,

Human supremacists, just to watch the two grind each other down. Then the Rio Alliance could be free, and maybe expand to include dozens of new species, instead of the main four they represented at present.

"What about me?" Remahle Mebarsu asked. "I can do his job just as well."

Lazarus had to agree. Most of the cargo on *Shiva Zephyr Glaive* had come in one or two square cubic foot boxes, heavy enough that he was the only one who could simply lift things and put them atop stacks. On *Ajax*, the boxes tended to be huge by comparison, designed to be carried in even larger standard containers.

At the same time, there were cranes and waldo arms that Remahle could drive just as easy as anybody else, which let the four-foot-tall glider squirrel of a Kr'mari handle big loads by himself.

"I suspect that I'll be too busy with other things," Lazarus said carefully to him. "That means you'll have to step up to take one of the loadmaster jobs, just as Aileen has had to become a full quartermaster."

Her fur ruffled with pride when he said that, but it was God's honest truth. Lazarus had never met anybody with such an intuitive ability to rearrange forty boxes, in her head, to get the perfect fit, with the things needed most at the front, on the first try. *Ajax* was mostly empty now, but at some point, they would get home, and if he could keep her as crew, there would be five hundred Humans serving here, plus whatever diplomatic mission they hopefully asked him to carry back to Innruld space.

It was going to be an utter revolution when he did return. Not just bringing eight new species with him, nine if you counted the two robots: Cormac the NavCrawler and Lenox the MedCrawler.

No, somewhere in High Command was a spy. High

enough placed that they had been able to tell Westphalia exactly where to go, and where to hide, to ambush *Ajax* when he came out of jump.

They had come that close to killing him.

Lazarus took that just a little personally.

TWO

ADDISON

IT WAS SHIP'S EVENING, and Addison had joined Lazarus in the man's office for a chat. Eha had joined them, in her capacity as a senior member of the Species Underground, rather than maybe Addison's current girlfriend and potentially-future mate.

The room betrayed the person Lazarus had been before, matching the name on the wall outside: Francisco Luiz Oliveira, Capitão De Mar E Guerra.

Walls had been vertically paneled with a dark wood. Carpet had even been laid, which had been utterly weird to slither over, entering across the threshold. A wooden desk had been centered in the room, with the first chair Lazarus would find comfortable in five months, while the Human had removed the two on this side.

Addison and Eha would be comfortable coiled for now. And Addison needed this to be something of a private conversation. Ereshkiki Nisab had been his second-in-command, back on *Shiva Zephyr Glaive*, but he just wanted to be a Systems Mechanic, not a rebel. As long as the two could be pried apart.

"So we're proposing revolution?" Eha asked carefully as she settled onto her coil.

She was the outsider here. Lazarus had been with his crew long enough that they had threatened to quit if Addison had turned the Human over to this woman. Paranoia, perhaps, but the gendarmes had staged a raid, just as he was coiling to talk to Eha back there, and they had all blasted their way out of Zhoonarrim Station and presumably into a life of crime.

"That's one way to look at it," Lazarus replied just as carefully. "The Rio Alliance is just barely holding its own against Westphalia. *Ajax* could tip things back in our favor. At the same time, the Innruld, while they dominate in your sectors, are not powerful enough to fight either side in my sectors. Knowledge of Innruld space will get out, and merchants, pirates, and spies can be expected to go looking."

"What about the rest of Rio's navy?" Addison asked. "I know *Ajax* is something new, but what about the average pirate? Can they slither in and set themselves up as new overlords by displacing the Innruld ruling now?"

Addison appreciated the way Lazarus sat back in his chair and let his eyes come unfocused as he processed.

"The average merchant will be about as well-armed as *Shiva Zephyr Glaive*," the Human said after a few moments. "The technology is different, but beam weapons and ray shielding are comparable there. It's in the drives that you'll have a problem."

"You've carefully not ever discussed how *Ajax* moves," Addison pointed out.

"I never knew it was possible to travel so slowly through FTL space that you could notice it, Addison," Lazarus leaned forward again and they locked eyes. "*Ajax* uses star drives, rather than trans-space generators like you have."

"Meaning?"

"Meaning I lock estimated coordinates and jump, and I'm there between ticks of an atomic clock," Lazarus said.

Addison's scales flexed outward with dread.

Yes, that could be dangerous, if you could outrun the police so quickly that you could land somewhere, pivot, and escape before they waddled up to capture you.

"Accuracy becomes the key element then, because I'm jumping in a straight line on a vector," Lazarus continued. "*Shiva Zephyr Glaive* can turn in trans-space, navigating around stars in the Phraettis Nebula along a secret path, so it's really just one long jump for you. I would need to make five or maybe seven, depending on how cautious I was feeling. I'd still move faster than you on your best day. The pirates will be the same way. As would rebel starships if the Rio Alliance provided you some."

Rebel starships.

Addison's scales felt like they were standing on end. Eha certainly felt it as well, because he was holding her hand and felt the flinch pass through her fingers.

Warships that could fight the Innruld overlords? And not just armed merchantmen that might be able to survive an encounter with one of the Security Barcs? Actual, purpose-built warships?

Lazarus had said that he could easily have annihilated even something as heavily armed as Zhoonarrim Station with *Ajax*'s guns.

Could the Species Underground break the Innruld?

That had been the dream, possibly for as long as the Innruld had been in control of the others, some two thousand years now.

Addison flashed to the overlords in his memory.

Legend had it that they had bred themselves for beauty. There was some truth to that.

Seven feet tall, generally, although lean and elegant,

weighing perhaps just a little more than Lazarus did. The same erect biped design with incredibly long arms and legs mated to a long torso.

Skin on an Innruld was just darker than cream, where Lazarus was a few shades darker and covered over, at least his top half, with freckles. The overlords of the galaxy usually had blond fur atop their head, long and fine, compared to the much shorter, orange hair Lazarus had, and his eyes had whites around the pupil, where the Innruld's were a solid, bluish gold.

Beautiful, perhaps, in the same way that a marble statue can be beautiful. Cold and aloof, at least when dealing with what they considered all the lesser species, which was all of them.

And they had structured an entire galactic culture to serve them, with the Innruld on the topmost tier of caste. Below them, all the various servants: the police, the bureaucrats, the thugs who were granted some level of benefits, in trade for keeping their boots on the necks of the rest of the galaxy, those people just trying to make an honest living and maybe save up enough for the occasional vacation.

It was enough to drive a young Churquen into radicalization.

Thirty years later, it was enough to keep a mature, rational ship's Director just as angry as he had once been.

Addison nodded.

"All of this is just speculation, Lazarus," Addison said. "Rebel starships for the Species Underground would be lovely, but pardon me if I need to see them first."

"Understood," the Human replied. "My superiors might not see it the same way as you and I do."

Addison wondered if Lazarus would rebel against order at that point. Especially if the other Humans resisted.

"So first," Addison finally said, "we have to get you home safely, Lazarus. How?"

"I've been giving that a lot of thought over the last few weeks," the Human commander replied, turning dark and broody compared to his usual disposition. "I can't trust anyone outside this ship right now, for obvious reasons, so we need to make a few quiet stops between here and there."

"What are you going to do?" Eha spoke up again.

"We're going to commit a little piracy."

THREE

EHA

IT HAD BEEN AN INTERESTING QUESTION, pushed off until now by circumstances, but Eha found herself in an interesting and slightly unwelcome conundrum tonight.

Aboard *Shiva Zephyr Glaive*, she had been a guest. Addison had put her up in one of the spare cabins, fitted out for the occasional passenger he might carry, not all that far from where the Human slept.

Not all of her nights had been spent there, once she had come to realize that Addison was too intimidated to actually approach her for any sort of relationship beyond the professional one they had maintained for the last decade.

Spymaster and spy.

So she had had to provoke him to step outside himself. The impressive Addison Wolcott, tongue-tied by a woman. Who would have ever guessed?

But now, they were on an alien warship, commanded by someone else. Addison could just be himself, if he remembered how.

Eha could pretend to be a civilian. It wasn't who she was, but it was close enough for now. She might even enjoy the project enough to make it a full-time gig, as the chances were that her cover was completely blown in Innruld space at this point.

Everything had all come down to the question of cabins.

Lazarus already had his own space, from when he had first launched this impressive monster of a craft into space. There were crew quarters scattered around, but mostly at the two ends of the vessel, where seven hundred Humans could be maintained, with the vast majority of those tripling up in a single cabin.

Lazarus had explained to her the concept of hot-bunking, and she supposed it made sense if this was a military vessel. Any one of the three crew members assigned to a room might be on duty at any given moment, with another sleeping, and the third doing whatever maintenance you needed to do when you were a uniformed sailor, rather than a cargo pirate like Addison's crew had been. It would not be all that crowded in the room.

In addition, there were two score cabins for officers and senior enlisted people, who rated a space to themselves.

Addison's crew rattled around in here like the noisemaker her kind had once developed on their tails, before losing it later. Small rock, big space.

Lazarus had looked at her with steely determination in those strange, round pupils and assigned her to a cabin alone.

She had been similarly situated on *Shiva Zephyr Glaive*, but things had been different there. She had rarely slept alone during the last two weeks aboard the freighter, spending her nights entwined with Addison.

Now, this team was facing the most important thing since the Species Underground had been founded. The chance to actually find allies capable of breaking the Innruld and their hold on known space.

All Eha could think about right now was whether or not she wanted to sleep alone tonight.

After a lifetime given to the movement, with all that risk and danger, wasn't she due a little happiness? She had never *joined*. Never *brooded* a new generation of young. While she wasn't too old to consider it now, she had the necessary chemicals in her system to prevent it, as long as she continued to take them.

She could enjoy herself. And Addison.

And maybe be free. Hadn't Lazarus described this trip as a beginning?

All her freedom would end when they dropped out of trans-space in a Rio Alliance system. At that point, Eha Dunham would have to become an Ambassador to the aliens. A representative to the Humans, who potentially contained enough power within themselves to overturn thousands of years of history.

Or conquer the entire galaxy by themselves.

The shiver rippled down her scales like a small earthquake, clear to the pointed tip of her tail.

Addison was already committed to whatever course of action Lazarus would undertake. His crew had accepted the Human as one of their own, in spite of everything. Or maybe because of it.

She was the outsider here. She would need to approach this with a clear mind and open eyes, lest Addison be swept up by…something.

Avarice? Revenge? Glory?

At one point, she had been convinced the Human was a charlatan. A confidence artist using the cover of a lost sailor to prepare Innruld space for invasion by learning all their soft scales.

That was before *Ajax*.

Eha had traveled to more places, and more planetary

cultures, than probably all of Addison's crew combined, as she knew they generally stayed to the lower class docks and only worked on a small edge of Innruld space.

She had seen bigger vessels, but those were the massive Command Pyramids that the Innruld used to travel in extreme state between castles. *Ajax* was larger than any Security Barc she had ever met.

If Lazarus was right, even the Command Pyramids would be easily defeated, if not destroyed.

Would the Humans free them when they arrived, or conquer?

The Innruld had ruled for two thousand or more years, thwarting all the other species and keeping those numbers small and fragmented, as to benefit the long-living and slow-breeding overlords.

Humans would arrive like a plague.

She had to prepare for them, but Eha had spent decades preparing. One of the long-term projects the Underground had actually gamed out was how to take a First Contact with another species and parlay that into power. She'd seen the reports, but nobody had ever expected a more advanced species in greater numbers and capable of the level of casual violence and strength that Lazarus of Bethany represented.

Tonight, however, she didn't have to be on stage. She could be herself, whoever the real Eha Dunham had turned into over the last three decades.

The future would arrive soon enough, and the chains around her coils would bind her again, after just a taste of personal freedom that she had denied herself for so long.

Eha looked around the cabin one last time. Chair for a biped to sit and presumably read, too tiny and uncomfortable for her to do more than vaguely drape herself across. Desk inset into the wall across from the bed, where someone could presumably work in a spindly metal chair. Bed tucked against the other wall, again designed for Lazarus and not a Churquen, although she was confident she could coil herself in such a way as to sleep more or less comfortably. Drawers inset into a wall for clothing and personal effects. Inset closet next to that for pants she didn't need to hang, or a heavy jacket she had traveled without.

She had fled with nothing but her shirt, her vest, and her harness. All of those would have fit into a drawer, but at least the Necherle mechanic had taught himself how to sew clothing for Humans. Anything for a Churquen was far easier, so she had enough clothes to get through her days.

And Thadrakho was making her something formal with which to meet Humans.

But that was tomorrow.

In her first night on an alien ship, Eha didn't want to be alone.

She turned to the main hatch and opened it, surprising Addison as he was about to knock.

Perhaps he also sought solace?

She noted that he held a bundle of what looked like blankets in his hands as he slithered closer.

And all his scales had flared out in abject embarrassment as she smiled at him.

Addison gulped once and stared at her for a long moment.

"Would you like some company?" he asked in a tiny voice.

"I was just coming to knock on your door," Eha replied.

More flare of scales, this time almost halfway down his coil. She had never imagined this man as shy or awkward.

Eha slithered back into her cabin and gestured him to join her.

"The closet contains an extra blanket," he said by way of

introduction as he did. "With the one from the bed, I wondered if we might make a comfortable nest."

Eha smiled at the man and moved to the closet, locating the identical bundle and pulling it down. The room would be crowded, at least until they found a place to store the chair, but four blankets on the floor would provide sufficient cushion against metal deck plates.

Quickly they arranged themselves on the floor in a cozy nest and twined their coils.

"I worry about the future," Addison admitted as they lay tangled. "Up until now, I generally had control of my life, being Director of my own ship. But now I am nothing but a passenger, as you and Lazarus will make all the important decisions."

"You have described him as a friend," Eha offered, staring deeply into his eyes for cues about his mental health, not just as a spymaster, but as a lover and a friend.

"Hopefully, he views us the same way," Addison replied. "Everything is out of my coil now."

"Not everything," Eha reminded him. "The crew will look to you, rather than him, for direction, if things get messy and complicated. I will, as well."

"I work for you, Eha," he said. "Have for more than a decade."

"And I would have eventually done the foolish thing and demanded you turn him over to us for interrogation. That would have been the greatest mistake anyone could have made."

"*Ajax*," Addison nodded.

"Exactly," she said. "We have at our fingertips the future of all species, and not just the Innruld."

"I fear Humans," he admitted in a low voice. "I fear their potential for violence. I fear their technology. I fear for our place in their universe."

"It would have arrived eventually, as you yourself have noted while arguing in favor of this trip," she pointed out to him. "At least now, we may be able to generate positive outcomes."

Just to make her point, Eha also kissed the man whose legendary reserve and dignity hid depths of concern for propriety about their relationship. She would need to cure him of that, as well.

Another task for another day. Tonight, she would experience that fleeting sense of freedom, before duty awoke on the morrow.

FOUR

AILEEN

AS QUARTERMASTER, Aileen was responsible for all supplies on this vessel. As Loadmaster on *Shiva Zephyr Glaive*, it had been largely the same, but the scales here wanted to intimidate her.

If she would let them.

Just add a couple of zeroes to everything and move forward.

She could only imagine what it would be like when Lazarus had a crew greater than just them. When hundreds of Humans might come to rely on her for their daily needs. That would make her an officer. Did she want that?

Aileen wasn't sure. It would probably get in the way of her being able to work magic on the loading deck, cramming more things in than anyone imagined.

But if she wasn't in charge, someone else would be. Some fool with a clipboard.

Some *bureaucrat*.

She tried not to roll her eyes too hard at that, lest she pull something.

She had returned to the aft section of the ship by way of

a slidewalk that seemed to be like ice under her feet, except it was metal when she stayed still. Only when she moved did she glide.

Lazarus had shown her the technique for movement, describing it as ice skating, where you somehow pushed off at an angle with one foot and then the other, and the machines pushed back and held you a hair above the deck itself.

Quick way to move. Awkward the first time, but with a half mile to cover, she had learned the trick.

Most of the supplies were back here, stored around and in the bases of those three, enormous fins, one hundred and twenty degrees apart, that held the engines and weapons systems.

But she had a special responsibility. One that Lazarus had impressed upon her, the two of them making the first journey alone.

He had taken ninety-eight sailors into space with him on that first voyage, the one that ended in battle and flight. Twenty-eight of them had remained aboard when the others surrendered to the Westphalian GunWall.

Their bodies were still here.

What did it say about a military ship that they had enough cold storage space to carry that many corpses at the same time?

She and Lazarus had talked about burial in space for the men and women. Innruld space vessels only went to great effort for the overlords themselves. The rest were wrapped up in a piece of cloth and jettisoned, maybe with a ceremony, maybe not.

But Lazarus had wanted to haul them all home. To not leave them in so-called *Alien Space* for all time.

She supposed he felt an enormous guilt at being the cause of their deaths. Aileen had seen it in his eyes, his shoulders. It had not mattered that these men and women were all volunteers, according to Lazarus. He should have been able to protect them.

Now, they were her responsibility.

Aileen wasn't morbid enough to actually check on the bodies directly, after that first time where Lazarus had shown her what he had done.

Twenty-eight bodies, dressed in new uniforms and placed on cold-storage racks in a separate compartment from where food was kept frozen. Because this was a warship, and you were expecting to haul dead people around.

Tonight, she needed to check that the equipment had not malfunctioned. That the temperatures remained a few degrees below freezing. That all the food in the refrigerator and freezer was still good for now.

Aileen Enjehn. Loadmaster. Quartermaster. Maybe pirate.

And keeper of the corpses of *Ajax*'s first crew.

Lazarus had explained to her why Humans consumed poison. Alcohol wasn't deadly to them, like it was to everyone else. Some alcohols, anyway.

Lazarus drank it because it was slightly poisonous. Just enough to loosen the muscles and the mind. To help you relax when the weight of all the universe was pressing down on you in a lost warship seeking troubled skies.

As Aileen completed her checklist and headed towards her cabin, she would have liked a good, stiff drink of...something.

FIVE

LAZARUS

IT HAD TAKEN A SECOND WEEK, but Lazarus wasn't in any hurry. They had enough food aboard *Ajax* to feed this tiny crew for nearly a year if they were careful. And every day they sat parked was that much closer to *Ajax* being as repaired as the ship could get without returning to the graving locks for things.

Already, his ship could kill everything he'd seen in Innruld space. And do significant damage to anything Westphalia might send his way. Once he got a proper crew trained, even a full GunWall would learn to fear them.

The hardest part, looking around his bridge, had been drilling the deck plates so that he could install seating for non-bipeds. The floor here on the bridge was already set up for Human stations to move around, following standard configurations.

He'd have liked to have had a chat with the fool who had never considered coil nests for the two Churquen, a squatting stand for a Vaadwig, a nest for an Ilount, or a docking station for a NavCrawler. But that was also him, back when he was just *Pancho* Oliveira.

When this was only a Human endeavor.

Before Innruld space.

Before *Lazarus of Bethany*.

"Pilot, prepare to break orbit," Lazarus said in a loud voice, even though Kuei was only ten feet away.

The moment was building up inside him and he was having a hard time pretending that it was just another day at the office.

Kuei seemed to sense that. Her station was next to Wybert, and both glanced over inner shoulders at him.

At least they were both grinning, although most Humans wouldn't be able to see that in the way Wybert's antenna wiggled, or Kuei's ears came forward.

"Standing by," Kuei replied after a moment.

"Fusilier, confirm your status," Lazarus continued.

Wybert panicked, but Lazarus had an identical screen in front of him, trusting that Kuei had her job handled. More importantly, nothing Wybert did right now would accidentally fire a beam.

Shiva Zephyr Glaive was the only thing around to lock weapons onto, at the moment, and a Star Spear would blast that ship into glowing fragments at this range. Lazarus didn't feel the need to buy Addison a new ship, just because Wybert was being Wybert.

"Uhm, all systems show green," Wybert eventually managed, his antenna going flat sideways in embarrassment.

"This is why we train, Fusilier," Lazarus said warmly. "Habits in peace become habits in war. If you do it enough times, it becomes so automatic that you don't make mistakes by overthinking things."

Like an owl, an Ilount's head could rotate one hundred and sixty degrees each direction. The first time Wybert had turned like that, Lazarus had nearly leapt out of his skin, but it was second nature now to just glance up from his boards and smile.

"Really?" Wybert asked in awe. "That's the secret?"

Lazarus nodded. He supposed that Wybert, like all Ilount males, had been kicked out of the nest at the rough equivalent of fourteen and left to fend for himself. Most died pretty quickly as a result, but the Queen only needed one male to mate with every five years, and kept a few older ones around for their wisdom and experience, as well as backup in case no new candidates stepped forward.

Only heroes got the opportunity to mate with a queen. Wybert of Capantzina was no hero, but he had also lived far longer than most of his broodmates, lucking into safe employment with Addison where his destructive tendencies could be channeled.

"That's the secret, Wybert," Lazarus assured him. "Spend an hour every day practicing slowly and then building up your speed once your muscles know the movements."

"Huh."

The head turned back and around and the antennae returned to vertical. Lazarus shared a grin and a nod with Addison, seated off to one side as kind of a First Officer In Training, along with Eha, the Ambassador he was transporting to his home system.

"Pilot, accelerate one quarter and come about starboard when we clear the planet," Lazarus said. "I have designated a target on your boards as *Aleph*. Center us enough that the weapons can bear."

Lazarus took a deep breath as Kuei pressed buttons. Everything seemed to flicker a little as the generators handled the surge. Inertial dampers and artificial gravity would keep everything more or less stable as they moved, and the ship was riding friction on gravity waves, rather than using a chemical or electromagnetic thrust for propulsion.

The feeling in space wasn't all that different from driving a boat underneath the surface of an ocean, which had been the basis for much of the ancient leap into space in the first place. Self-contained. Able to handle extreme environments. Things you had to look at on screens rather than with an eyeball, both underwater and in space where four hundred miles was close battle range.

"Engaging," Kuei replied as the ship broke free into space.

This gas giant had a plethora of moons in semi-random orbits, some of them just captured iceballs that would eventually hit others and explode into rings, but with the ray shields up, they'd be safe enough to get clear of the larger moons.

Addison and Eha had remained silent up until now, watching carefully as the Rio Alliance Navy went to work with two new recruits here on the bridge and several more aft. Addison already knew how to command, but Lazarus needed to train him to sound like a naval officer, so that folks back home would treat him like one.

"Is everything announced and repeated?" Addison asked querulously.

"Indeed," Lazarus smiled over at him. "Loud enough that everyone on the bridge might hear it, in case they need to react, such as a sensors officer reacting to new zones of clearance as the ship crests a horizon. The person executing the order repeats it back so the officer knows that it was understood the first time, or if they should clarify it. Again, habits in peace that make the place noisier than hell in battle, but everyone can follow reasonably well."

"Humans are a strange species, Lazarus," Addison remarked.

"It will get worse, my friend, before it gets better," he replied with a smile.

Lazarus pushed a button on his console and opened a channel to the engineering bays where the rest of his crew were monitoring things. Ereshkiki Nisab and Thadrakho were smart, and learning, but his previous Engineer had spent two decades in the fleet, learning the old power systems, and the last five years adapting to the new designs Lazarus and others had come up with when dreaming up *Ajax*.

"Engineering here," Ereshkiki Nisab replied with three voices.

"How is our power output holding?" Lazarus asked.

Like with Wybert, he had a series of readouts stacked down the side of his screen to monitor, but Ereshkiki Nisab had a much better understanding of what he was doing.

"Far better than I would expect, given the damage you had supposedly sustained," Ereshkiki Nisab said. "There are no leaks for Thadrakho to fix right now. I'm not sure how to handle ourselves down here."

"I'm sure that will change soon enough," Lazarus said with a laugh that everyone on the bridge shared.

Shiva Zephyr Glaive was always leaking somewhere. Or shorting. Something. Thadrakho was constantly inside repairing it, or building a replacement part.

Ajax would be the same way, but they had just spent days cleaning filters and lines, so everything should behave for a bit longer. Later, it would get exciting.

"Pilot, bring up a rear view on the main screen," Lazarus said. "Lock on *Shiva Zephyr Glaive* and magnify."

Everyone had personal screens, but there was a monstrous projection on the front of the bridge where things could be shared without anyone needing to unbuckle and move. *Shiva Zephyr Glaive* appeared now, asymmetrical like a treble clef flying in space, slowly receding as *Ajax* powered up and out of orbit.

Lazarus had originally placed his ship in a spot where the various gravity wells would hold it for at least a decade, so Addison's ship would be safe there, assuming nobody stumbled across it while they were gone.

All the water had been drained from the tanks into *Ajax*, so nobody would be taking it far if they did, unless they wanted to refill everything first.

Addison's eyes were rapt on the screen when Lazarus looked over, but Eha was studying him instead. Made sense, he supposed. It wasn't her ship, except in that she had been Addison's superior officer in the underground.

She wasn't in Lazarus's chain of command. He just smiled back at her, willing to grant her Ambassadorial status for now, while Addison figured out what he wanted to do.

Pancho Oliveira would be returning home, after all. And maybe he'd get a hero's welcome. Maybe not.

He had no idea if the spy who had sold him to Westphalia might be in a position to brand him a traitor. But bringing potential new allied species would go a long ways towards defeating that sort of sentiment as well.

Addison was the one Lazarus trusted, not Eha. Addison's crew had made him welcome, accepted him. Everything.

Eha was a spy. Not necessarily a spy for anyone bad, but someone who of necessity lied for a living, and Lazarus would need to peel those layers back carefully and see what she was really all about. He couldn't necessarily trust Addison's judgment there, either, as the man had confessed a long crush on the woman and was finally acting upon it.

Besotted or not, he was compromised in his emotional judgment. But Lazarus knew that. And he had the rest of the crew to fall back on, if something important came up.

Aileen, for example, didn't bend. If the Churquen got weird, he'd let her step in and speak, as she'd known Addison for many years.

But that was just his own paranoia speaking and Lazarus understood that. He smiled at Eha, and she returned it. Nobody here knew his face well enough to read his thoughts, especially not her.

Well, Aileen probably could by now, but that was the benefit of working with him daily for several months, as opposed to just eating meals together, as he had with most of the rest of the crew.

Time passed as everybody settled into the normalcy of space flight.

"We have cleared the planet and Target Aleph is on the centerline," Kuei announced. "Current distance one thousand, two hundred miles and closing slowly."

"On the main screen," Lazarus ordered.

Right at the edge of where the normal Star Lance could engage, and even then it wouldn't be all that accurate. Deadly, but fairly random.

Ajax wasn't going to use one of her Star Lance beams.

His ship was bigger than any of the GunWall vessels, and didn't have that huge defensive rim around the bow like a Viking shield. Didn't have the articulated joint at the center where the engines could be rotated in a variety of directions to maneuver while keeping the wall itself and all the guns pointed at an enemy.

The Westphalian GunWall moved and fought as an entity.

Ajax had *Kirov's Lance* instead.

The target today was one of the outer moons of the gas giant. Sensors had shown it as a rock ball with an icy surface that might have been a world-girdling ocean, closer to the distant sun.

"Fusilier, lock on Target Aleph with the Lance," Lazarus said slowly and carefully.

With any luck, his calmness might accidentally infect Wybert. Pigs might fly first, but anything was possible.

The Ilount looked down and clacked his four mandibles together as he worked. Again, not that complicated a task for the person shooting. Most of the work was done by the pilot and the engineers to bring the bow onto the target.

"Target locked," Wybert finally said. "I think."

"You think or you know?" Lazarus fired back at him.

The head rotated and Lazarus could see panic in the back of all five eyes, but Wybert blinked really hard and flinched all four arms together in such a way that the ripple went all the way aft to his spinnerets.

"I know," he said after a long moment. "Target acquired and locked."

"Engineering, prepare to fire the Lance," Lazarus said as he opened a channel to the whole ship and left it for everyone who wanted to hear. "Fusilier, fire."

Wybert's upper arms were stronger, designed to hold his powerspear or lift things. They weren't as well designed or capable as a Human's, but it worked for an Ilount. And Wybert usually used his lower pair of arms for finer manipulations, so it was almost a shock when his top, right hand stabbed at the screen in front of him.

Except that he had been watching training videos made by Humans, for Humans, and they didn't have the extra pair of arms coming out just above their hip bones.

On the screen, Kirov's Lance fired.

Ajax had far more power systems than the ship's mass required. Channeling it through the ray shields and engines had kept him alive during her first battle. Today, all that energy had gone into a ring of capacitors around the neck of the ship, just behind the front of the big fins aft.

Every one of them dumped in a rapid sequence, lased

into coherence at the midsection and then the bow, and leapt across space.

The moon erupted into a huge cloud of plasma as the beam shut down.

"Recharge the beam, Director?" Wybert asked immediately, sounding almost like a man who knew what he was doing.

"Negative, Fusilier," Lazarus replied automatically. "Route extra energy into ray shields."

"Aye aye, sir."

Lacking a sensors officer, Lazarus was handling that himself today, although Kuei probably could have done it. He wanted her focused on flying this strange new vessel.

The moon was a rock that had been hit with a cutting laser, as the cloud of plasma and debris cooled and expanded into adjacent space. The shot hadn't hit square, so they had also introduced a wobble to the tidally-locked rock that would probably take decades or centuries to taper off.

And that moon was ringing like a bell right now.

Lazarus smiled. He'd never had a chance to fire the Lance during that first battle. It took time to charge, and he'd been fighting defensively for his life, using the three Star Lances on the engine pylons to engage the GunWall.

He knew what it was intended to do. Kirov had designed the prototype and gotten the approvals to build a ship around the design, which was when a captain with a hard science engineering background named *Pancho* Oliveira had come in.

Ajax had resulted.

But it had never been fired in battle.

"Wow," Wybert whistled in awe.

Looking over from his seat, Lazarus saw that the Ilount had managed to echo Lazarus's screen on the side of his own, so he could see what he had just done to an innocent moon.

"Pilot, new bearing up and port," Lazarus said. "Get me clear of all the orbital debris and into deep space so we can start our journey out of the nebula."

"Up and port," Kuei replied. "Stand by."

"Lazarus, that's…" Addison said from the side.

He had also been following along on his own screen. His pupils had opened all the way and his jaw had fallen open. Presumably shock.

"You asked what *Ajax* was capable of, Addison," Lazarus said firmly, pointing at the screen. "That."

"What would have happened had that been Zhoonarrim Station?" Addison asked.

His tone wasn't accusatory, so much as fearful.

"Blown it into a billion pieces, Addison," Lazarus said. "Hopefully, when the war comes, that won't be necessary."

Lazarus understood the man's nervousness. Nothing the Innruld possessed could stop Kirov's Lance. One GunWall ship would turn to gas, but they were rarely lined up enough for a single shot to pass through and kill a second. However, Westphalia had bigger things than a GunWall and *Ajax* was designed for them as well.

And hopefully, the Innruld would understand, although Lazarus supposed that he would probably have to demonstrate things at least once.

After that, maybe the *former* Overlords of the Galaxy would understand.

SIX

LAZARUS

IT HAD TAKEN them three days to navigate their way out of the nebula, and Kuei needed the practice calculating corners when she was used to a ship that could turn in transspace and fly doglegs. They were in open space now.

The Phraettis Nebula looked like a shield across a wide arc of sky when viewed from Brasilia, his homeworld and the capital of the Rio Alliance. From this close, it was a lumpy blob of newly-born stars and gas clouds that seemed a solid wall of tapioca pearls in milk on most screens.

He had gone there to die. Expected to.

But he had emerged reborn. Lazarus smiled, alone on the bridge for now, with Kuei and most of the rest asleep. Cormac the NavCrawler could keep the watch, but Lazarus had been in the Navy far too long to be comfortable without someone on the bridge. Cormac could handle most things, but Lazarus wasn't used to a machine that was as Human as the rest of them.

He was surprised when Eha opened the aft hatch and slithered onto the bridge. He had been expecting her to be with Addison, but maybe she had put him to sleep so the two of them could talk.

"Cormac, I would appreciate time to have a private conversation with Lazarus," she said to the NavCrawler as she reached her coil nest and settled in.

"Cormac, why don't you move down to the auxiliary bridge and I'll transfer control to you when you arrive," Lazarus offered, trying to make mental amends for not treating him like a full crew member.

Addison and Kuei did. Sentient computer systems were still a taboo subject back home.

"*Very good*," Cormac replied, unplugging himself from the simple i/o interface Thadrakho had worked up and tracking across the bridge to the hatch.

They were alone.

Lazarus had been expecting this conversation. He knew all the others well enough to understand their cares and concerns, including Addison. Most just wanted to be safe and productive.

Eha was the representative of something greater than just a cargo runner's crew.

Lazarus programmed a control to beep when Cormac was ready for command.

"Good evening, Eha," Lazarus began, as if they hadn't all just eaten dinner together a few hours ago.

"Hello, Lazarus," she replied. "We need to talk."

Lazarus kept the grin off his face. Back home, a woman started a conversation off that way when she was about to dump you. Or at least give you the ultimatum of quitting her or quitting the Navy.

Lazarus had never married after that.

He nodded for her to continue.

"Are you really planning to overthrow the entire galaxy, Lazarus?" she asked bluntly.

He was a little taken aback, but only by the ferocity of her words, however mildly she might have spoken.

But she was right. He could see that in the way she phrased it. *Ajax* was intended to push Westphalia all the way back. To win that war against the Human supremacists. Nothing the Innruld had was capable of stopping a fleet of warships from either Westphalia or the Rio Alliance. The many species of Innruld space would almost be innocent bystanders caught up in the storm.

"I hadn't planned it that way, Eha, no," he said after a moment to process all the implications. "The Rio Alliance wants peace, but Westphalia is intent on conquest. We would have fought all our wars in ignorance of you folks, and then eventually stumbled across an Innruld vessel of some sort, maybe a free trader like Addison."

"What would have been the outcome?" she asked.

"Depends on who would have won the original war," Lazarus said. "The Rio Alliance would hopefully welcome even more non-Humans into the fold. Westphalia would have probably put you on reservations without access to space, to eventually wither and die."

"And now?"

Lazarus shrugged, a gesture common to both species.

"Now, I want to sneak home and see who our spy is," he said. "Introduce you folks to my superiors and see what we can do to establish trade. To make the galaxy a better place."

"But you fear your own kind."

She hadn't asked a question so much as stated the thing that haunted Lazarus's dreams when he tried to sleep. Like why he was on the bridge in the middle of the night.

"How did the authorities on Zhoonarrim Station know to raid that tea shop while we were all there?" Lazarus deflected the conversation back onto her.

"A leak," she replied, nodding in acknowledgment. "Perhaps a spy feeding the authorities information."

"Just so," he said. "Someone told Westphalia how to find me. Where. When. If I just sail up to headquarters to say hello, all of you are at risk of spies or assassins."

"You still haven't answered my original question," Eha said. "Does all of this necessitate overthrowing the entire galaxy? Innruld, Rio, and Westphalia?"

"Do you have an alternative, Eha Dunham?" Lazarus asked. "Innruld know the Humans exist, but not where to find them. At least not yet. Addison and his crew know much more. I can work as a pirate for a short time, but this ship was never intended to operate that way for long. When we arrive somewhere, news of new species will ripple out. The galaxy will have to change. At that point, the only question is how much."

"I have pledged my life to overthrowing the Innruld and their hold on all the other species," she said. "Why could you and Addison not just recruit a crew of non-Humans and do that? Why do you need to return home first?"

"Why not just leave the non-Humans behind then?" he countered without any heat. "Sail back someplace safe and pretend I never heard of Churquen? I have no more love for Innruld than you do, Eha. But that culture has been stable for centuries, and nothing is going to change much. The Rio Alliance is being pushed back by Westphalia now, so I need to return to fight. The others chose to come with me, including yourself."

He paused to study her face. It wasn't as expressive as a Human's, covered over as it was with scales, but he had spent enough time around Addison now to see some play of emotions around the eyes and how the scales on the cheeks moved.

"What are you truly afraid of, Eha?" he asked in a quieter voice.

"Humans have the power to completely overwhelm Innruld space, Lazarus," she said quietly. "To turn into another set of overlords, and one we could not cast off, not without finding another set of space-bound wizards with even greater technology to do the job."

"Humans are coming," Lazarus said. "It is only a matter of time. Your luck was that I came first, and came now, rather than an exploration fleet in a century or three, when our technology was even more advanced, since the Innruld prefer everything static."

"Can you guarantee that the Rio Alliance will welcome us?" she snapped. "Accept us as full members? Allies? And not just the next crop of peasants?"

"Rio? Yes," he said. "That's what the Rio Alliance is. Humans, Moah, Gnashiiley, and Atomarsk working together for a common good. Churquen, Ilount, Vaadwig, Yithadreph and the others should be part of that. *We hold these truths to be self-evident that all sentient creatures are created equal, that they are endowed by their Creator with certain inalienable rights, that among these are life, liberty, and the pursuit of happiness.* Those are the words from our Founding, Eha. They are the Rio Alliance."

She nodded, falling silent.

"I hope you're right, Lazarus of Bethany," she said.

He didn't know what to say as she slithered off her coil and made her way to the hatch and opened it.

"I hope you are right."

SEVEN

ADDISON

ADDISON HAD NEVER IMAGINED the power that a ship like *Ajax* represented. The casual capability for destruction frightened him, even when Lazarus had felt comfortable enough to leave a nervous Churquen in charge.

But they were making greater speed across the cosmos than Addison had believed possible, even making single jumps and recalculating the next stop when they determined where the gravity depths of the galaxy had shifted them.

You opened a hole in the universe and stepped through.

Awe-inspiring. Frightening.

According to what Addison had read, the ship emerged from such a jump with a flash of brilliant azure light that was a collected blueshift, so you had to announce your arrival in a grand way, as opposed to just slipping out of a trans-light tunnel at your destination politely.

This was going to change everything. Hopefully, the Churquen would be able to survive such a flood and prosper, even if they didn't swim worth a damn. Too much hinged on his coils now.

Addison looked over at Lazarus from the station where

he was commanding. They had left the Human console in place, since Lazarus would continue to command later, but Addison was going to be in charge for now and his console was just as good as any other.

All he lacked was to be seated directly behind Kuei and Wybert. And he understood why Lazarus was hesitant to take Wybert with him on his mission.

But for a very brief time, the dangerous warship *Ajax* would be commanded by non-Humans. Flown by non-Humans. Even, Gods save them all, fought by non-Humans, if it came to that.

"You'll be okay?" Lazarus asked.

Again.

Addison nodded, understanding the Human's unvoiced concern: what would Addison do with a ship like this while he was gone?

"We will be fine, my friend," Addison reassured him.

Again.

"Just make sure that you completely destroy the Innruld if it comes to that," Lazarus said.

Addison nodded.

They had plans in place, the two of them. If something happened to the thing that Lazarus called a Mission Team, and the worst resulted, Addison was to take *Ajax* back into Innruld space and start his revolution. Nothing there would be able to resist him, and Addison had the contacts to recruit enough of a crew to do the job.

Going the other way, the Rio Alliance might welcome a group of unknown aliens flying *Ajax* home to them, but Addison and his crew would be quickly separated from such a powerful vessel and probably held as some sort of prisoners for a while.

Whether Addison told the Humans the truth at that point would come down to how destructive he was feeling.

"Go," Addison commanded the Human. "We will be fine here, patrolling slowly and training carefully while we await your news."

He watched Lazarus nod to himself once before he finally turned and walked out of the room rather than speak again.

Aileen had shared some of the things she knew about Lazarus, and the return to *Ajax*, so Addison understood the potential for guilt that the man carried. Anything might happen out here, but Addison knew that he would be safer running at the first hint of trouble, even possessing a death-beam like Kirov's Lance.

He did look forward to meeting that Human, Kirov, one of these days, just to perhaps better understand a mind dedicated solely to finding ways to kill and destroy.

And Wybert would be upset that he couldn't play with such a thing.

Addison was just fine hiding.

EIGHT

LAZARUS

THE TWO WOMEN were already aboard the pincke when he arrived in the landing bay and boarded the vessel.

The term *pincke* was ancient, going back to maritime sailing on Earth itself and referred to an ancient class of flat-bottomed ships with shallow draughts and large cargo capacities that allowed them to serve in a variety of circumstances. Originally a Dutch word, it had somehow come into space to describe the standard cargo shuttle that almost everyone used, the only differences generally being the interior furnishings, and which of the two front seats was for the primary pilot.

It was long and narrow. Bigger than the koch and with all the space dedicated to cargo, rather than transporting Humans in any sort of comfort. In fact, the only nod to convenience was a small head, tucked forward behind the cockpit, opposite a pantry and kitchenette. If you wanted to sleep on a pincke, you either racked out on the deck, or hung a hammock from one of the many hooks available.

Aileen was already strapped down in the co-pilot's seat today, with Eha coiled across and around a jumpseat she had pulled down as an anchor. Both were dressed in what Lazarus had requested as second-best clothing. Tan capris and a blue vest for Aileen. Eha had a rust-colored shirt and her usual harness with pockets and hooks.

Both women looked a little silly with standard issue Rio Alliance Navy pistol holsters on, but Lazarus wasn't about to let them go anywhere without at least a Manticore-brand light laser pistol. His own Ares was much heavier, but both alien women could handle a Manticore in combat if they had to shoot something.

Nobody but Humans and Kreeghal had the shoulders to handle anything heavier for long anyway.

"Status?" Lazarus asked Aileen as he buckled himself in.

"Pre-flight complete and we're ready for departure," Aileen smiled up at him with all of her whiskers today.

Completing a basic familiarization course for certification with the pincke had been a requirement, before Lazarus would ever let her fly one. He only had two, and no easy way to repair them if something happened.

"You take us out," Lazarus decided. "I'll handle communications."

Immediately, she moved her hands to the flight controls, a two-handed yoke like an ancient ground vehicle, but with buttons and levers everywhere you could reach.

"*Ajax*, this is Shuttle Number One, prepared for departure," Lazarus said.

"You have clear skies, Shuttle One," Kuei replied brightly. "*Ajax* is secured for flight operations."

After two weeks, she even sounded like a Rio Alliance pilot. He made a note to tell someone how useful all the basic training videos were, when you needed to train a new crew in a hurry. Hopefully, the bosses would let him keep his friends aboard and supplement them with others, instead of grounding him for piracy and everything else.

Of course, *Ajax* was more dangerous than any ship in the Rio Alliance fleet, too, if it came to that, but he thrust such thoughts from his mind and concentrated on the first step of his return to friendly space.

"Unlocking docking cradle," Aileen called out in a slow, measured cadence as her hands moved. "Powering up maneuvering thrusters. Soft contact only confirmed. Detachment confirmed. Stand by for powered flight."

Lazarus was poised to step in and override, but she was handling it like a pro so he began to breathe easier. A quick glance back at Eha confirmed that she was just as nervous, so maybe it was okay.

The pincke turned away from the big ship and aimed like an arrow at a star in the near distance.

"*Ajax*, this is Shuttle One," Lazarus called. "Stand by for redshift."

Aileen glanced over and the look in her eyes was a strange combination of apprehension and excitement. That made sense, as she was about to do something nobody she knew had ever done, fly a shuttle with star drives.

"Engaging," she said breathlessly as a furry hand came down and pulled the levers into contact.

Pincke Shuttle One blinked out of the universe.

NINE

AILEEN

WOW. Just like that, and they were gone. Aileen wanted to pinch herself to be sure, but all the stars out the forward portal were different than they had been just a moment ago.

Even the space around them tasted blue.

Aileen smiled over at Lazarus and winked.

"Arrival at primary destination," she said. "Confirm coordinates."

That was his job, since he had let her fly. And she had just traveled through trans-space so fast that nobody saw it. Opened a portal and went zip.

This was going to change everything, once these sorts of things were available in Innruld space. Or whatever people started calling it after the tall shits who used to be in charge got knocked off their pedestal of beauty.

Aileen had never intended to be a revolutionary. Nor a rebel against the supposed natural order of things.

She was just a puzzle-solver who wanted to travel in space instead of settling down and having kits. Revolutionary had come later, when it became clear that the Innruld ruled and everyone else served. And that Addison Wolcott was more than he seemed.

Aileen supposed she should probably feel some level of guilt or remorse for the lives she had helped destroy, but they were Innruld lives. The Overlords of Everything. And the drugs she helped the Underground deliver weren't useful against anybody else.

And the Innruld really did deserve it.

So what did that say about what was coming next?

Humans.

Addison might have his doubts, but not Aileen. The Innruld stood about as much chance as a fart in a spacesuit. Stinky and rude, but not really going to do much to everyone else.

"Coordinates confirmed," Lazarus replied as she sat and considered whether or not Aileen Enjehn was evil.

Or rather, how evil she was.

The Innruld were doomed. She would have done it slowly. One of those boxes at a time. Grind down lives into chemical dependency. Let the overlords slowly breed themselves out of existence over the next century.

The Humans were going to do that much, much faster. And a lot of it would be her fault.

She could have spoken up. Or rather, not spoken up. Not challenged Addison when Eha called for him to deliver the Human to her and her masters. Not threatened to quit, along with everyone else, if anything happened to Lazarus.

Not called Addison's bluff.

Aileen kept her thoughts to herself and her whiskers forward as she calculated the next step on their flight. She'd been planning on handling sensors and nav today, with Lazarus flying, so she took it as a compliment from the man that he thought she could do it all.

Maybe next time, she'd have the ship to herself and could fly it anywhere she wanted.

Where did she want?

Aileen wasn't sure.

"Current coordinates are off by about eight light-minutes," Aileen said aloud.

"And that's better than expected with a pincke on a jump of this distance," he replied. "Usual error factor is thirty light-minutes when you jump that many centuries."

Centuries? *Light*-centuries?

She'd lost track, overwhelmed by just jumping.

Aileen spun the map back to a larger area view, until she saw the system where *Ajax* was waiting for them.

Crap. All that, and we've just jumped farther than the long axis of Innruld space, too?

She kept her muttering inside her head and dialed things back down.

"We're going here?" she asked, stabbing a spot on the screen with a stubby, furry finger so like his, and yet so different. "A pirate base?"

"We don't know that it's a pirate base, Aileen," Lazarus reminded her. "It's just an outpost well outside Rio Alliance space on the far side from Westphalia. And it handles an amazing amount of traffic for the tiny population in the system."

"Smugglers," she said.

"Probably," he grinned back. "If you're outside of certain legal boundaries, you aren't paying taxes on things, and if your cargo is big enough, that's worth the time and consumables to make that sort of round trip."

"And you trust the sort of folks we'll find there?" Eha asked from the backseat, just before Aileen could.

"About as far as I could throw them," Lazarus replied.

That took her a moment. Yithadreph didn't throw things like Humans apparently could. Her shoulders didn't have the rotation of his, or the musculature. She certainly couldn't throw a small rock at one hundred miles an hour, like Humans reportedly could.

But Humans weren't *that* strong. Lazarus was using a euphemism for not very far.

She could grasp that. Lazarus had proven to be a stand-up being. The rest were criminal scum. Emphasis on the scum part, since she had criminal covered herself.

"But we want information from people you don't trust, as well as possibly recruiting crew members?" Eha asked, still a little put out.

But Little Miss Perfect back there wasn't used to not being in charge. Must rankle her fur, scales, whatever, to have to take orders from someone else. Aileen grinned where the spymaster couldn't see it.

"I've been gone for half a year," Lazarus said. "News of the battle might have made it this far out, but I'm more interested in learning what else we've missed. I can't imagine that the Rio Alliance has won the war, or lost it, but things change. Especially with what happened to *Ajax*."

"Your spy might have done more damage?" Eha asked. "Enough?"

Aileen watched Lazarus shrug those enormous shoulders and turn back to study the Churquen woman.

"I don't know," he said honestly. "Maybe. We can't just land at Brasilia to ask, without knowing if the rest of you would be welcome."

"And yet you only brought us two?" Eha asked, causing Aileen's ruff to stand up a little.

"Aileen is stronger than she looks," Lazarus said. "And both of you are smarter than I am, at least when it comes to the sort of street smarts we'll need at a place like Yisan."

Aileen felt her ears go back and her whiskers press flat. Humans apparently blushed by turning red in the face, but Lazarus had spent too much time around her, because he grinned. That just made it worse.

"Bad?" Eha asked.

"It is a wretched place, from everything I've heard," Lazarus said, his expressive face screwed a little sideways as he turned his head fully to engage the spy. "Everything is available for sale on the docks, if you have enough cash and people don't think you are a cop."

"Then why not bring the rest?" she asked.

Aileen had heard the story. Hell, Eha had, but she just presumed the other woman wanted to talk through her own misgivings.

"Wybert would get into a fight if he was here, so he shouldn't be here," Lazarus said. "That means Addison needs to stay back and keep a watch on the Ilount. That means *Ajax*. It cascades from there, but you two are needed the least to maintain my ship, so you're free. And you've got the skills I need. Cargo and espionage."

Aileen shrugged in turn. Lazarus was right. She knew the docks better than anyone on the crew, and he'd said that Zhoonarrim Station wasn't all that different from Tershuvi Port, on the surface of Yisan. She'd shoot first if it came to that, and then argue legalisms with Humans later.

Assuming Lazarus didn't do it first. He could be violent when he wanted, just like he could get the rough spots on her spine with his nails when she needed it.

They made a pretty good team. Eha would bring her own skills and sensibilities, but she was going to be all about overthrowing the Innruld, so it would flavor her swim.

Aileen shrugged again, internally, and lined up the star she wanted on the viewer and locked it in. This would be about three jumps, unless she got dead lucky with the first one, but she wasn't trying to get that close to Yisan from here. Just into the system where they could look around and see what the smugglers were up to.

She was, after all, already an expert at smuggling.

TEN

EHA

FROM ORBIT, Eha wasn't all that impressed with the planet. Maybe a little stormier than some of them she had looked at. It was an oceanic world for the most part, apparently similar to the Human home world, but with even less dry land.

Churquen didn't swim, but the city was located a little inland on a protected bay, so she had little fear of having to get near that much water. No, it was still the Humans she would need to fear.

Lazarus had explained that about half of the Humans would see her as some sort of animal, even after she spoke, betraying their own Westphalian background. The others would most likely be trying to get coordinates out of her so that they could be the first to arrive on an alien world, either for trade or predation.

She knew how to use the pistol she wore. The technology was different, but the physics of an opposable thumb grip and a trigger were universal among bipeds, and she qualified for her top half.

And her tail could always wrap around some fool tight

enough to break bones or strangle them. Her kind hadn't evolved with poison to kill their prey.

Humans were especially strange in having ports like this on the surface of a planet, rather than in space, but she wasn't trying to change them. This ship would land on the surface of Yisan at a place called Tershuvi and make a modified First Contact. Information and maybe some trade, whatever could fit into the aft cargo section safely, if anything presented itself.

Information was still central, though.

Up until now, all the stories of the Rio Alliance and Westphalia had been filtered through a single Human. She had no reason to doubt him now, not after actually flying aboard *Ajax* and watching the man nearly shatter a small moon with that terrible weapon.

But she needed to see how the rest of Human space saw itself.

Innruld space was stable in a three-tiered cake. The Overlords themselves in the Innruld. Below that, their bureaucrats in all the various flavors and responsibilities. Then the combined collection of all the other species.

Eha hadn't probed Lazarus too deeply for similar socio-economics of his home, so much as listened to the things he said and the places he talked about. Brilliant child from poverty elevated by education to prosper in the Rio Alliance military.

What would these people be like? At Zhoonarrim or Dormell, smugglers were usually one or two steps above the bottom of things, preying on the weakest for the strong. At best, they were evading the law to give the little people something that might provide some manner of escape from the drudgery of their everyday lives, but only at a terrible cost that might not be evident until much later. Like those six boxes she had caused Addison to transport to Dormell, Aceanx, and Zhoonarrim.

Yes, Eha Dunham understood smugglers. That snide smile they all developed after a while, if they weren't dedicated to a higher calling, like Addison Wolcott. The sass in the eyes when they knew they were putting one over on the system that they nominally served.

What would Human smugglers be like? If she had to classify Lazarus as a hero, then the rest probably fell into a zone she understood all too well.

Back home, that made them the easiest to seduce or blackmail, with mind or body, if they weren't careful about their lives.

"Stand by for landing," Aileen said a little too loud.

From the tone, Eha assumed the Yithadreph woman was terminally insulted to be landing on a planet without any sort of traffic controls in place. After all, orbital space was huge, but there was still the risk of two vessels unable to maneuver well and trapped on intersecting vectors.

But Yisan was a smuggler's paradise, and those sorts really didn't believe in even the littlest amount of laws and structures that would make life better for everyone.

The Tragedy of the Commons, where everyone preyed on everyone else, rather than working towards a harmonious whole. In that, Aileen would classify the smugglers not much better than the Innruld on almost anything.

Eha could work with that.

ELEVEN

LAZARUS

ONE OF THE reasons Lazarus had picked Yisan in the first place, over places closer to the line that would get him home, was that the surface gravity was so low compared to standard G. About ninety percent, which would be just a little heavier than the two women were used to, but not enough to seriously compromise them in the short term.

Addison had explained that Churquen didn't swim worth a damn, but he wasn't planning on going out on the water anyway, and he had Aileen if things got hairy. He could swim, but Aileen was as close to a Dire Otter as you could get. Her cabin on *Ajax* had been completely redone so she slept at night in her own wading pool.

She'd be fine on Yisan.

"Landing imminent," Aileen called as the pincke began the last few feet of descent on oxygen/hydrogen thrusters, the pincke itself engulfed in a fog of hot steam. "Fifteen feet. Ten. Five. Three. Contact."

Lazarus had his hands poised to override, but she was probably landing better than he could right now, both eyes on the screen as the bottom radar watched the ground come up, and both hands delicately adjusting as a strong crosswind off the ocean wanted to push them off the center of the pad.

She was an absolute natural. But he knew that. It was just another of the reasons he felt safe with Aileen and Eha with him, rather than any of the others.

Outside, the weather was just pissing down rain, but that wouldn't really impact anything. It did, however, remind him that his two companions were used to living aboard a starship or stations, where there was no such thing as weather.

Thankfully, Thadrakho had planned ahead.

The pincke settled and Aileen powered everything down according to the exact textbook. He might not have done as good a job, but it had been years since Lazarus had flown with any regularity.

"Landed and secured," she said aloud.

He nearly laughed at the sour look that came over her face as she looked out the front windshield and registered the slashing rain. If anything, Eha would be worse off, but they didn't have to leave immediately.

"Local meteorological report says it should pass in about thirty minutes or so, and then we've got the rest of the afternoon with a high pressure front overhead," Lazarus said helpfully. "That means clear and warm enough."

She turned her glower in his direction and he grinned.

"You'll be fine," he continued. "A little wet and that's only a maybe. Your shoes will handle it. Eha has to slither around puddles, you know."

She relented, but he could see the growl in her eyes.

"I'm going to make myself some coffee," Lazarus unbuckled and rose. "Would you like any?"

Without a crew consuming it, *Ajax* had nearly two tons

of coffee beans down in the freezer. More than he could go through in his lifetime, maybe. None of the new crew liked the hit of jitteriness that accompanied the caffeine, but Lazarus was in heaven again, able to work first thing in the morning instead of feeling his way to coherence.

"I would like some," Eha said. "Extra thin."

Lazarus headed aft to the kitchenette and got to work. He would make himself a full batch that was a little extra-strong and pour some into a mug for the Churquen woman and cut it seventy percent with hot water, until it wasn't much more than a pale tea by comparison.

But it also wouldn't make her jumpy.

They sat and drank in companionable silence. Aileen took a few sips from his mug, as he had expected, but otherwise didn't like the stuff. More for him.

Eventually, the storm front passed. Outside, the pressure rose rapidly and the sun came out, turning everything just a little muggy.

Aileen was dressed for it, with an extra jacket Thadrakho had made up for her in a waterproof material close enough to cotton duck. Eha had something like an opera cape, long in the middle to cover a little of her coil but shorter on the sides so as to not drag in the mud when she moved.

Lazarus had reverted to the reds today. He even had his original jacket, that bright crimson with the beer company logo for Lunatic Alchemist Brewing on the back.

Anyone in space who had ever been into an emergency pack, for any reason, would probably recognize that logo. Here, it would mark him as more of a refugee than a naval officer.

Hopefully, that would distract folks from the truth. And lend credence to his story of how he came across two new alien species nobody here had ever heard of.

They emerged into the early afternoon sun and Lazarus took a deep breath of the first natural air he had breathed in more than a year, with so much time in the graving dock getting *Ajax* ready to finally fly.

Aileen emerged next, and then Eha, and he looked around.

Tershuvi Port didn't have a tram service that ran in a nice loop for sailors who didn't want to walk. Nobody here was willing to pay for it, or for the taxes to support something so civil. And the pincke didn't have any sort of land vehicle they could have hopped into and run about in, although Lazarus could see buying or stealing something if he was going to take his time getting back to Brasilia.

He shouldn't dawdle, but the list of people who had known where *Ajax* was going to come out, and when, wasn't that long, and most of them were *Almirantes* of some sort, or extremely senior politicians who should have been above reproach.

Somewhere, a bad apple threatened the entire barrel. So he was on Yisan, walking across the packed turf and gravel beds of the port. It was only about a half mile to the main terminal itself, and he had programmed the pincke to only respond to the three of them and nobody else, so that ship was safe.

And he had access to funds from *Ajax*, so they weren't impoverished either. Lazarus just had to be careful, in the middle of a place he could charitably call a pirate haven, when he was Rio Alliance Navy, about as close to the cops as most of the people he would encounter on this planet would ever get.

He smiled and sauntered. Aileen had stubby legs, and Eha could only slither so fast, so it was more of a stroll than anything. At least it had been pouring rain, and most folks were inside, so he wouldn't make much more of a scene than necessary.

After all, nobody on this planet had ever met a Yithadreph or a Churquen.

At least, not yet.

TWELVE

AILEEN

SHE KNEW BETTER, but Aileen was still horribly insulted at how poorly this port was run. She was used to stations, where you docked according to rules and fees. Officials with clipboards—*CLIPBOARDS!!!*—met you before anything could be moved from the cargo deck.

Organization.

Addison had been a smuggler, not a pirate, so they hadn't ever had to visit places like this. For a reason.

The surface under her feet as they walked was compressed gravel. Only the landing pads themselves were stable, usually either hardened concrete or cut stone. And it was apparently warm enough for grass to grow in strange clumps, although not any trees anywhere close to what she could see.

She already knew there was enough water to support them.

And the ships around here…

In Innruld space, most of the system-hauling ships never entered the atmosphere, leaving that work to local vessels or specialized shuttles like the pincke. *Shiva Zephyr Glaive* was a clockwise coil of a ship. You didn't have to have symmetry.

Everything she could see was sleek and symmetrical down the centerline.

And boring. Mundane.

She wanted art in her marine architecture. Elegance. Design.

Pirates apparently made lousy artists.

They moved close to the main building, what Lazarus had called the terminal.

Again, nothing like Zhoonarrim Station, with the lower decks for working folks and then moving up to the spires of the Innruld in Skycity. Here, she could see a variety of buildings, but most of them had the look of warehouses, at least farther out.

Closer in, everything looked like bars and shops.

The bad parts of a system concourse, when you took a wrong turn and ended up down in the places where you had to occasionally pull a knife on someone.

Or, in her case, a pistol. Stupid, drunk Humans looking for trouble would get shot out of hand, and she could always claim ignorance of their laws. Or say she was defending her honor against a rapist, whatever the stupid, furless bastard had actually said.

If he wasn't around to give testimony, he couldn't call her a liar later.

You tall assholes keep that in mind.

"You're growling," Lazarus said quietly out of the corner of his mouth.

They had ended up walking side by side, with Eha a pace behind.

"Sorry." Aileen felt her whiskers pull flat against her face.

"I'll shoot first," he offered.

And he would. Aileen knew Lazarus felt an extra layer of protective over all of them. Alien, true, but also women, and his culture had some sort of masculine overtones that said women were to be cherished and safe, or you weren't a man.

Silly, but she would take advantage of that.

They came to a powered door made of something transparent and heavy. It slid to the side with a thump as they entered sensor range and Lazarus stepped through first.

Aileen had to tap it with a knuckle as she crossed the threshold.

"Silicon based?" she asked him as he had stepped to the side to wait.

"Safety glass, yes," he said. "Silicon-based and refined with heat to a very stable form, covered over with a layer of polymer to keep it from scratching and hold shards when it shatters. Cheap to make and incredibly durable."

"Huh," Aileen reponded.

The weird shit you could do on a planet, when you didn't have to plan for pressure failures.

Inside, the place looked more like a station. They were in a big foyer, surrounded by shops that seemed to be mostly bars, occasionally with some food, and at least one bodega. Escalators took the visitor to a second and third floor, with mezzanine balconies overlooking and presumably containing other shops.

The noise hadn't fallen completely silent, but Aileen could see the ripples of heads suddenly turning this way to stare at her and Eha.

One spacer had been in the process of exiting the facility when they entered, and had staggered to a halt about fifteen feet away. Humans apparently came in just about every color of skin that you could imagine, as this one was much darker than Lazarus, almost the color of old wood that has been handled so much that oils had turned it nearly black. And his hair was matte black.

The cut of his clothing was almost identical to Lazarus's,

so she knew this had come from a Human emergency pack, or been cut to the same, cheap standards. Green pants and jacket in a dark sage almost the color of the sorts of dangerous mold you got if a room got too wet and sealed up for too long. Black leather boots to knee, matching belt, matching holster. White shirt with buttons up the center of the front.

He just stared at her.

"You got a problem, pal?" Aileen snapped at the tall Human, giving the punk her best stinkeye.

The man did something Aileen had never seen before when Eha slithered into the hallway. An honest-to-goodness quadruple take. It was almost like someone was gigging him in the tail with an electric prod, to watch his eyes surge and his shoulders quake.

Their eyes locked and then his fell.

Lazarus had told her that she was morphologically close to a Human female, at least compared to the rest of the crew. They'd be taller, with impossible legs and similar curves through the torso, minus all the fur. But with breasts. Two of them, situated more or less how a Yithadreph did, under her vest and jacket.

Stupid punk was staring at her chest. Like a teenage Yithadreph boy. Although she occasionally caught Lazarus doing the same thing. Must be a male function.

"I'm talking to you," she growled, causing his eyes to come back up to meet hers with a shock so plain she nearly laughed at him. "Move along."

She made a rude gesture Lazarus had taught her, and the Human staggered backwards, turning and scampering back towards the nearest bar.

Presumably, whatever entertainment he had back on his ship wasn't about to match what he expected inside this shopping mall.

She looked up at Lazarus and caught the shrug.

Yeah, he knew. Freaks on parade, at least until everyone understood that there were whole other species out there they'd never heard of.

Eha had gone cold. Aileen could see all of her scales lying flat against her skin right now, but she took a breath and almost smiled at Lazarus.

"Who's the lucky publican?" she asked.

"Not following that fool," Aileen gestured at the spacer's back as he moved.

Lazarus stood in place for a moment, turning his head right to left and then back, up a level.

"Food," he said. "There's a dim sum place on two that should be safe for both of you to eat."

Aileen fell in behind him, one hand just resting on the butt of her pistol on general principle. Anyone staring too long got the stinkeye, but nobody walked any closer or made any sort of threatening moves.

That was good. She might be a little too keyed up right now.

Up the escalator, they turned left and walked almost all the way back to the front of the mall to the front door of a restaurant. A Human behind the tall lectern waited with eyes wider than was probably comfortable, and a jaw hanging slack.

"Three for lunch," Lazarus said companionably as they got close.

The Human was frozen, like prey trapped in a bright light.

Aileen figured it must be a female, based on descriptions Lazarus had provided. Furless. Weaker bones in the face. Bigger eyes. Skin a burnished gold with hints of yellow underneath. Narrower shoulders and waist flaring out to hips. Legs out of proportion to even Lazarus, as he had said. Breasts.

She wore a black skirt that looked impossible to even walk fast in, let alone do any work. Cream-colored blouse looked pretty enough. Those shoes must be a torture device invented by someone who hated women. Who would voluntarily stand on their toes with six-inch heels all day?

Eventually, the woman's brain caught up with the day and she grabbed menus. Obviously on autopilot, as she turned with a *Right this way* and led them into the restaurant.

It would be too much to ask to be put in a quiet corner, and Aileen knew it. Plus, neither she nor Eha would be comfortable in what Lazarus had called booths.

Human morphology architecture assuming stupidly-long legs and no tail.

So they ended up at a table in the middle of the room, like performers on a stage. Lazarus did not appear concerned.

"We'll need one booster seat and no chairs on that side," he said calmly.

The woman was clueless, but a Human male in black slacks and apron over a white shirt appeared immediately and got to work, seating them, providing water in clear mugs that also seemed to be made of glass, from the way it thunked under her thumb.

At least the smells in here were appetizing. Everyone else in the place had fallen into the sorts of dread silence you got when somebody farted loudly in a theater.

She could do this. Lazarus had chosen her, because the docks were her expertise.

She could do this.

THIRTEEN

LAZARUS

SO FAR, so good. They had made a splash, pretended it was nothing at all, and made their way into a Chinese restaurant. Not a traditional one, but one of the tourist versions that had conquered all of Earth and then most of Human space after colonizing the North American continent and adapting to non-Chinese palates.

Proper Sino food was much spicier than a place like this would generally serve, and while he rather preferred that, all the extra spices were something of a crapshoot for his two crewmates and friends, and he didn't need the extra risk that it would entail. Vegetables cooked in fairly bland sauces. Meats breaded or not and served in small communal bowls. Egg rolls.

All things they had tried aboard *Ajax* from cold stores and been able to eat.

Lazarus was even going to be nice today and not order wine with dinner. Much as he missed it.

The waiter got them settled like he did this every day and returned with a pot of steeping tea and three mugs.

Aileen was on a booster chair that put her up where she

could see the room better. Eha was coiled up on herself across the table, more or less in the center of her side where nobody walking by was likely to step on her tail accidentally.

Lazarus had chosen this joint from the Gazetteer because it was part of a chain that spanned big chunks of Human space, even pirate outposts like this one, and served a standard menu from ingredients shipped in freezer pods nearly half the size of the pincke parked outside. The tea would be adequate. The food would be boring but safe.

The chances of a bar fight breaking out were much closer to zero here than at some of the places on the ground floor.

Interestingly, the lady at the front had instinctively grabbed the tourist menus with the pictures next to every dish. Everything was in Interlac, but somethings didn't translate well out of Romanized Chinese, and neither of the women knew many names of things.

The waiter returned after a few minutes, the star of a show where everyone in here had stopped talking, possibly stopped breathing, and turned to just stare.

Eha rotated her head to look up at the man and blinked calmly as he gulped in nervousness.

"Sweet and sour chicken," she said simply. "The dinner, and not just the plate. With a shrimp eggroll on the side. Egg drop soup."

Lazarus kept a scowl of seriousness on his face, but inward laughed as the man twitched once, and then fell back onto his professionalism, writing everything as fast as he could onto a small pad of paper.

"Madam?" he turned to Aileen next, probably guessing based on her shape as much as anything.

"Kung pao chicken, number two spicy, please," she said in a bright voice that only had a trace of Innruld accent in it. "Won ton soup."

Again, the gulp. Never dealt with two aliens like these

before, and they had apparently eaten Human food enough to order at a restaurant without his help. The waiter turned to him now and Lazarus could see the whites of the man's eyes.

"I'll have the Mixed Special Chow Mein," Lazarus said, unable to pick just one protein today. "Two chicken egg rolls on the side."

"Very good," the waiter said, disappearing in the direction of the kitchen like the Devil himself was in pursuit.

Around them, a low rumble of conversation picked up, heavy on shocked whispers. Lazarus turned to scan the whole place, watching people blush and fall silent as he stared at them.

Unlike more civilized places, there were few families in here, even with it being a middle-class kind of restaurant on the surface of a planet. He supposed that the locals had their own places to eat, well away from the starport and the sorts of folks drawn to Yisan.

No, most of the people in here had the look of officers off some vessel, or owner-operators flying tramp freight and making enough that they didn't have to settle for the noodle shops and pasta joints below.

He wondered who would be the first to try to join them. A restaurant like this didn't commend itself to someone just walking up and sitting down, and there were no spare chairs unless you brought your own. However, they would retire to the lounge later and enjoy more tea, which was when he expected someone to recognize the beer logo on his back and come to *rescue the poor sailor from penury.*

Or some similar song and dance.

They waited in companionable silence, broken by low murmurs back and forth but nothing of any great importance.

Soup was first, served with the traditional wide spoons in

small bowls. It was a performance, and the women were up for it. Lazarus already knew Eha was a skilled actress, since that was a job requirement for a spy, but Aileen was handling herself quite well.

Food arrived next and the waiter was smart enough to bring forks with him. Lazarus was rather skilled at eating with *kuàizi* sticks, and he appreciated that the restaurant had elegant, lacquered sticks in black, rather than the simple bamboo rods you broke into two pieces before eating.

Not that Aileen hadn't tried to learn eating that way, but she grasped the fork today and enjoyed things.

The food was better than a truck stop, to quote his father, but nothing to write home about. Everything came from closer in to the center of the Rio Alliance, delivered in big containers already prepared, to be warmed up and served here.

Lazarus was just fine with middle-class comfort food cooking today. It was about as good as he was used to from his time in the Navy and aboard *Ajax*, and it would make a safe-enough insertion into Human culture for the women.

He ate, watching eyes around the room and counting the number of folks working up the audacity to come over and introduce themselves. Nothing on his face invited such a conversation, so they kept their distance, many folks waiting well past the time they would have normally left, lingering over tea and rice wine.

Good enough. The interesting bits would come up soon.

FOURTEEN

EHA

EHA ATE DAINTILY. The food was actually rather good, once she got past the novelty of the taste and presentation. Lazarus had prepared them from the food stores on *Ajax*, and Khyaa'sha had selected the things she and Aileen could eat with the lowest risk of poisoning.

She had still taken things before she left the shuttle. Today's performance was too important to be sidelined by gastro-intestinal issues.

And it was a performance. Lazarus had warned them, but Eha already knew that she and Aileen would radically alter the balance of things across this whole periphery of space, just by appearing. Two new sentient species? Two?

Merchants and pirates would be drawn like flies to honey.

And she needed to make contacts out here. It wasn't enough to just talk to the Rio Alliance politicians. They might decide to make common cause with the Innruld to fight Westphalia, forgetting about all the other species under the yolk of the overlords, at least for a time.

She needed the criminals as well. The smugglers and

pirates that might decide to make their fortunes in Innruld space, regardless of what the Rio Alliance decided. It wouldn't take much to break the Innruld hold. There had just never been such an opportunity.

Eha had an eye to the main chance here. And as much as she respected Lazarus, she had her own species and the Species Underground to think about. If the Innruld could be broken, and the Humans prevented from stepping in to replace them, then all species might be free to pursue their own goals.

Churquen could expand to new planets and explore the galaxy. After all, Humans were only neighbors on one side, and that at something of a considerable distance.

What might she find if a Churquen ship went spinward and towards the core, where the stars were older and thicker? Were there other species out there that might help? Or, better, sectors with no higher life forms and planets that could be colonized?

All she had to do was break those chains for a generation, and they might never be replaced. Human technology would help, but she could not allow the Churquen to become reliant upon it.

There were just too many Humans. And they bred at a frighteningly prodigious rate. Eventually, they would probably conquer the galaxy, and perhaps the universe. Better that they be as fragmented in themselves as the servants of the Innruld were today.

But she smiled and kept her scales flexed appropriately as she made eye contact with other Humans around the space.

And a Gnashiiley, but a sub-breed she wasn't familiar with.

Back home, Gnashiiley generally had red fur on their heads and body, with that white patch around the mouth. Here, the man she was looking at had a darker coloration, gray-brown. He looked heavier, too, only a little shorter than Lazarus, perhaps, and built more rugged than she was used to.

In the shadows, he might pass as a small Human, if you missed the poofy tail and mistook the fur around his cheeks as a beard. And missed the snout.

Lazarus had called them *kitsune*, after a Human legend of a fox creature that turned into a man in the light of their solitary moon. This one was certainly radically different from the ones she knew. Bigger. Stronger.

Had they evolved fully into separate species, given the apparent isolation? Had these Gnashiiley escaped Innruld space at some distant past and fled into what would eventually be the Human zones, forgetting about the overlords?

Lazarus had not known about the Innruld, even though they had learned Interlac from the Gnashiiley and others.

Complicated. Perhaps the Gnashiiley, the Moah, and the Atomarsk were playing a long game to get Human strength to the point that they could smash the Innruld? If so, Eha supposed that they still felt the need to defeat Westphalia first.

She saw a few Humans around her wearing expressions of obvious disdain. Westphalians, she presumed, or perhaps just Human supremacists who would talk knowingly with the Innruld, were they ever to meet.

Eha found it terribly amusing when the waiter arrived with the check, glancing at each of them carefully before placing it closest to Lazarus. Bizarrely, it was paper, rather than a reader that you touched with your own to transfer funds.

But Eha supposed that there weren't recognized banks around here, and things would have to be done on either a local bank, which would take time, or the paper currency and notes of Westphalia or the Rio Alliance. They had arrived prepared.

Ajax had a store of such currency in a vault that Lazarus had shown her. Not enough to fund a war, but enough to handle crew needs and maintenance if something came up and they had to pay cash while arranging credit.

She truly was in alien space. Lazarus pulling paper from inside his jacket and handing it to the waiter was the thing that brought it home to her.

They had taken the first steps to their freedom.

Now came the hard part.

FIFTEEN

LAZARUS

TEA TIME. Or whatever Lazarus wanted to call it. They had moved from the main restaurant to the attached tea room, taking up space in a corner that had been cleared by management when Lazarus told the waiter his next step.

The two women were drinking non-caffeinated teas now, and Lazarus had ordered a small glass of wine for himself as a treat. Aileen had sniffed it carefully and then rolled her eyes at him, but he was expecting that.

Humans were about the only species that drank poisons like alcohol.

Some of the folks from the restaurant had moved to the tea room soon after they had, while others had apparently contacted their captains to come see.

It wasn't a zoo or a circus, but it probably would be by the time they departed to return to the ship, later this afternoon. Certainly, the place was far more full than it probably should have normally been on a Tuesday afternoon.

One gentleman was paying extra attention. He'd been over in the main room eating with what looked like some other captains, but they had not joined him over here.

Lazarus watched the man work up a good line to come over and introduce himself.

You would need one, given the circumstances. This wouldn't be just well-met strangers chatting.

Unless Lazarus chose to see it that way.

Still, the stranger rose. Asked a complicated series of questions with just the way his face moved, looking this direction.

Lazarus smiled ever so slightly in response and nodded. The man wanted to talk, but was willing to hold his patience until later, if necessary. At the same time, he didn't want someone else getting into whatever deals could be had without him taking a shot first.

Audacious, but polite. Refined even, to look at the man's clothing. Black slacks over black leather boots of a dressy kind. The dressy boots seemed to be an affectation, compared to the riding boots so many people wore

Instead of a jacket, like everyone else in here, he wore a hooded opera cape, black like his pants and lined with white silk. In contrast, he wore a canary yellow shirt that shimmered like silk. The holster on his thigh was the same polished leather of his belt and boots, but it didn't look worn and well-used, like some of the folks around here had.

Money. Flashy, but still discreet, managing that fine balancing act that didn't leave him looking like a clown or a pimp, when either option might have presented itself on a man without the reserves of dignity to pull this off.

He was Anglo, from the look as he approached. Roughly the same skin tone as Lazarus, without the freckles. Tall and slender, perhaps half a decade older than Lazarus, right at that point where a man's hair starts to come in gray instead and the beard suddenly goes white. Straight black hair kept short and dark eyes, but fairly light skin.

He approached with a highball glass of something caramel-colored with ice.

"May I join you?" he asked with a slight bow to the two women.

Lazarus noted that Eha nodded like a queen, while Aileen seemed to be measuring his net worth by his dental work and general haberdashery.

"Please," Lazarus gestured to the one spare chair left at the little table when they had sat down.

One empty chair at a square table meant you had to approach by yourself, without a wingman who obviously wouldn't have any place to sit, unless the strangers invited you to pull up a whole table, at which point others might attach themselves to the party.

Not that Lazarus hadn't gamed all of this out ahead of time. Certainly, he was probably the worst-dressed person in the room, but the scarlet jacket and beer logo had been a conscious choice, bait to see who would nibble.

The man pulled out the chair and seated himself with something just short of a flourish. Again, courtly manners, carefully studied yet subdued.

He had the look of a gambler about him, rather than a tramp captain. Hard, sure, but full of *bonhomie* and smiles as he sought out whatever marks he might induce to fund his lifestyle.

Lazarus smiled at the man and hoped he was reading the signals correctly.

"Oluchi Pryce," the man introduced himself. "I note from your fashion choices that you might have previously fallen on hard times, but seem to have landed in a bed of roses anyway."

"Indeed," Lazarus said, holding out a hand for the man to shake in the ancient pattern of two strangers demonstrating that they weren't holding a weapon. "Lazarus."

"Aileen Enjehn," she held out her hand and dared the Human to shake it.

Pryce did, gingerly. He might have shook hands with a Gnashiiley previously, and the feeling wouldn't be all that different, other than how small Aileen's hands were, and how calloused.

"Eha Dunham," the spymaster took her turn.

That was interesting to watch. Eha didn't generally appreciate physical contact, except with Addison, so shaking Pryce's hand wouldn't be her first choice.

She had, however, interviewed Lazarus extensively on Human conversational rituals on the way here, and on mating rituals so that she didn't accidentally cross any lines.

Accidentally.

Lazarus was sure there were folks out there that would fetishize her as a goddess, but hopefully none of them were on Yisan.

"What brings you to Yisan?" Pryce asked carefully, mostly keeping his eyes on Lazarus.

Probably so as not to gawk.

"Drive troubles," Lazarus replied ambiguously. "Shipwrecked, as you surmised, and then rescued. For the last half year I have been slowly working my way back to Rio Alliance space."

Slow being the part where he had first had to convince Addison to bring him as far as a warship more dangerous than anything in orbit or on the ground around here. Something so valuable that they couldn't even mention its existence.

"Are there any cargos on Yisan you might be interested in pursuing?" Pryce asked.

Lazarus smiled slightly. The man would have no idea what they had arrived in. And even knowing it was a pincke wouldn't give away too much, at least until he managed to contrive a way inside to realize that it was Rio Alliance Navy issue.

Why would alien women have such a ship? Or why hadn't Lazarus just jumped straight home?

Oh, the tangled webs we must weave.

"Information," Lazarus replied to the question. "I'm six months out of date on developments and carrying a cargo of such value already that I wanted to take the pulse of the galaxy before just arriving someplace."

Pryce's eyes went both ways quickly, studying the two women and somewhat awestruck. Humans generally only interacted with three alien species, as far as anyone knew, with rare sightings of a few others possibly.

Here were two more.

How many more might be out there, just waiting for someone to arrive?

Pryce took a breath and leaned back, as if casual. He sipped his drink to buy a little time.

"The war between Westphalia and Rio continues apace," he said. "Westphalia might be developing an edge, but they have not made much progress, except to pull more Rio ships off the frontiers. Criminal elements have taken advantage of the softening to grow more ambitious."

Lazarus nodded. About what he had expected, and news would be slow to filter this far, unless it was something grand, like a major battle. Hopefully, that meant that the ambush of *Ajax* hadn't rated. Or both sides were keeping things quiet.

After all, Lazarus had taken the ship and fled into the swamp, rather than destroy it. *Ajax* might yet still emerge, King Arthur returned from Avalon to wreak his vengeance.

"We have some cargo capacity," Lazarus offered. "Are there cargoes worth hauling as far as, say, Brasilia?"

Again, the flicker of the eyes. Transporting two alien women to the capital was a political statement. A measure of value that they were worth more than anything you might stuff in the back of a pincke.

"I'm sure something could be found," Pryce replied. "How long will you be in port?"

Lazarus shrugged.

Pryce turned to Eha and studied her a little more carefully. Lazarus nearly laughed at the cold, superior look she returned. Either she had studied his mannerisms closer than he realized, or that look transcended biology.

"If I may be so bold, madam, what species do you represent?" Pryce asked her.

"Churquen," Eha replied simply.

Pryce nodded and turned to Aileen.

"And you, Aileen Enjehn?" he asked, obviously having memorized both names.

"Yithadreph," Aileen smiled. "I would give you my card, but we left them on the ship, since you won't have the correct prefixes to deliver a message."

Pryce goggled for just a moment and Lazarus smiled. Maybe a touch overdone, but there was no doubting now that the two were intelligent, tool-using, and most importantly, technologically-sophisticated.

Not just a pair of semi-sentients that Lazarus had found and dressed up in modern clothing for an exhibition.

Still, Oluchi Pryce immediately produced his own—three of them—reaching into a pocket apparently inside his cape, and handed one to each, Lazarus being last.

"So you have had dinner and a bit of relaxation," Pryce ventured carefully. "What are your plans for social events while here? And how long had you intended to stay?"

"We have nothing firm, as yet," Lazarus replied. "Obviously, I have not had much chance to show the ladies Human society in any great depth. And Tershuvi doesn't necessarily recommend itself as a bastion of culture. Suggestions?"

"I myself was planning to engage in an evening of cards in a private room with some friends," Pryce said rather sideways. "Would the three of you perhaps be interested in joining as observers? The invitation usually includes a plus one, but I'm sure we can convince the hosts to stretch that, at least tonight."

Lazarus turned to the two woman and caught their reaction. Gambling wasn't something Addison's crew did to pass the time. Aileen was normally an introvert who retired to her cabin to read off-duty. And he really only knew Eha as a refugee on the run from the law, who spent much of her time with Addison.

Eha nodded, and then Aileen did a moment later.

"I think that would be capital idea," Lazarus said. "Where shall we meet you, and when?"

Pryce pulled back his left sleeve to reveal an antique-style, mechanical watch.

"Perhaps three and a half hours?" he replied. "Top of the nineteenth hour?"

He paused there, doing some interesting math in his head. Would he offer to meet them at their ship, and possibly try to get invited aboard to inspect it? Or would that likely push his new pals sideways and ruin his chances?

Oh so delicate, that math.

"The facility is private, and off-port," he finally said. "Perhaps we should meet at the front gate? I have arranged ground transport for myself there."

Lazarus nodded and slid his chair back to rise.

"Top of Nineteen, then," he smiled, shaking Pryce's hand as he rose.

The others joined in and suddenly Lazarus was departing, leading the three of them out of the tea shop and down the escalator.

Eyes and whispers followed them everywhere, but mostly people just gawked. And this was Yisan. It wasn't like there were port authorities worth the name that would suddenly show up and demand medical records for the two women.

As if that would mean anything. He had them, for the point when someone finally asked, but that would not be tonight.

Eha slithered close as they emerged into the afternoon's muggy sun. Aileen trailed.

"So what exactly are we in for?" she murmured.

"Up to a dozen Humans," Lazarus replied. "Probably mostly male, and successful businessmen, to be able to engage in high-stakes poker, which is what our friend seems to do. Private room with a bar and a small menu, unless this is a banquet facility, in which case they might have a full staff on hand. Games of cards, most likely. The rules are easy to learn, but mastering the psychology of play takes years."

"I see," she nodded. "And your purpose?"

"Identifying who might be the best candidate to give us information," Lazarus said. "I'd like to recruit a few crew members if possible. Rio Navy veterans who understand the equipment and can help Kuei and Ereshkiki Nisab run their departments. We can't fight anything with such a skeleton crew, and I'm nervous about getting deeper into Human space and needing to."

"Interesting," she drawled.

"And for you two, a chance to see Humans in a controlled setting, mostly ignoring you to pay attention to their game," Lazarus smiled back over his shoulder at Aileen.

"Plus, they'll be making all sorts of offers of credit and requests for favors, so you'll have some power to drive them as you wish."

"Are you going to play?" Aileen asked.

"I'm lousy at cards," he laughed. "Maybe chess, but I'm sure there are ringers out here as well. My goal is to watch, listen, and plan. You two should do the same, and try to enjoy yourselves as well."

Then they were back to the pincke. Lazarus checked all the settings, and the security system was intact. Breaking into a ship or stealing one were about the only capital offenses on Yisan. Everything else was usually good for a fine, but the locals didn't want to get a reputation as being anything less than safe for business.

Three hours, and then the crazy parts would begin.

SIXTEEN

AILEEN

IF THE OTHER two could do it, Aileen decided she could as well. It had been her plan to just retire to the shuttle without people breathing her air, but she should have known that something would ruin that idea.

Still, she was dressed well. Not like the Humans would have any clue what Yithadreph high fashion really looked like. She liked her capris and vests because they were comfortable and had enough pockets to store things on a ship. The jacket added even more pockets, and kept her clothes dry from any rain.

As if a Yithadreph cared about being wet.

The gun was an awkward addition to her wardrobe. It kept pulling her belt funny and almost making her walk with a stagger. Still, Lazarus had been right, when he said that nearly everybody they saw, not counting staff on duty in bars and restaurants, would be visibly armed.

Her guns just leveled the playing field, if someone wanted to get frisky. And some of the Humans she had seen today were as much bigger than Lazarus as he was to her, which was frightening. Aileen had never imagined Humans got that big. She didn't know a single species with that much variance within a single gender.

At least it had cooled down as the sun set. The air was turning crisp as they emerged and locked up the shuttle. Around them, more crews than normal seemed to be paying attention, standing around outside their own vessels for no reasons but voyeurism, presumably.

She smiled at a few of them, just because, walking along next to Lazarus and a stride in front of Eha. The Churquen was the real alien, being a non-biped covered with scales. Aileen was just a really big otter walking upright in fancy clothes, to see the Human records in the pincke's encyclopedia.

There were no catcalls, which Lazarus had warned them might happen if a Westphalian ship was parked here. Of course, Lazarus had also read the registrations of everything before picking a path to the front gate.

She had a pistol if she needed it. Aileen made her walk suggest that she knew how to use it.

The Human, Oluchi Pryce, was standing next to a long ground vehicle that rolled on black, rubber tires when they approached. A small mob of sightseers had gathered in the middle distance here as well, waiting for the show. Mostly it was a Human crowd, but she saw a few Gnashiiley and at least one Moah, the creature being shorter than her and rugged, and covered over with dark green scales, except a pattern of light yellow around the eyes of one and bright blue on the other.

No Atomarsk, which would have been awesome, as they were just legendary creatures in Innruld space.

Like the Gnashiiley, the two Moah were denser than the versions she knew from Innruld space. Maybe twenty pounds heavier on the same four foot frame. Not as tall as her, but maybe as strong.

She wondered if the Innruld were doing something to the species under their domain to keep them physically weak, as well as politically. The Gnashiiley and Moah here both looked more physically imposing than their cousins across the galaxy. They might also be able to help the Humans, but she wasn't sure what they might help the Humans do.

Free them? Or conquer them?

Aileen kept the shiver inside as they walked up to Oluchi Pryce.

The Human bowed formally to them with a flourish of the cape that looked natural.

"Good evening, my friends," he said with a smile as he straightened. "So glad you could join me."

"Our pleasure," Lazarus and Eha replied, almost in unison.

Pryce opened the door at the rear of the vehicle and Aileen went in first, sniffing everything. Two bench seats, facing each other. She found the latch and flipped up the one facing forward, just to make the two Humans look out the rear with her as they rode.

She slid all the way across and gestured to the open space when Eha entered next. The look of surprise on the woman's face turned to a sly smile they shared as she arranged her coils right in the middle of the back, like a queen facing her supplicants.

Lazarus entered next, sliding across with a grin and joining her.

Aileen watched carefully as Pryce ducked in, did a double take, and then ended up sitting next to Lazarus as he closed the vehicle's door. He thumped the panel behind them and the vehicle began to move, rolling noisily on the gravel and asphalt road.

"Thank you," Pryce repeated himself. "I expect that you are aware that you'll be the objects of discussion tonight. But

I know everyone there and can hopefully offer suggestions along the way."

"For me, this is more of a sociological expedition," Eha smiled. "See the Humans in something more like their native habitat."

Aileen grinned as she watched the effect of the words on Pryce. He wasn't a Human supremacist, but he also wasn't used to thinking of Humans as maybe being considered backwards by other species.

Looking at them, Aileen was struck by the coloration. Again, Humans apparently had a huge variance in such things. Lazarus had orange hair, while Pryce's was black and starting to gray. The newcomer's skin was much paler, even accounting for all the freckles on Lazarus's upper body.

Yithadreph fur tended to be within a few shades of brown, at least until old age set in and they started to turn gray all over.

They made polite small talk, but Eha deflected all the interesting questions, like where they were from, sometimes with nothing more than a peremptory smile. Eventually Pryce caught on and returned to safer ground, talking about Rio Alliance politics.

Aileen didn't follow it all, and wasn't that interested, so she let Eha and Lazarus probe this man for news and subtleties. Apparently, they got good stuff, to judge by the smiles when the vehicle rolled to a halt outside a wooden building that seemed to convey great age when she got out.

Pale blue walls on the large building's exterior, trimmed with white, seemed to have faded from something brighter. The roof was dark, but she didn't spend much time on planets to judge it for age.

Stations were either newly cleaned, or desperately in need of it.

The neighborhood was quiet and the best word Aileen could think of was rustic. Several multi-story houses around her, far too big for a single family, so she supposed they had been old money, built to impress, as Lazarus had said that only on new colonies did you get families with six or ten children.

Aileen couldn't imagine having six siblings. Her older sister Noreen was a happily-married housewife, raising one of her own, but Aileen had never wanted to settle down.

Or settle.

Oluchi Pryce led the three of them up the front steps with a grimace of apology at Eha, when Aileen was the one with the biggest trouble. Eight-inch risers were a pain for her short legs, and just brought home to her that Humans weren't nearly as gangly and awkward as they should be, with limbs so long.

A Human in a uniform of some sort seemed to be sort of guarding the front door. He wasn't armed, so maybe he was just a bouncer?

"Oluchi Pryce. I'm on the list tonight," he said as he approached, turning slightly to indicate them all with a grand sweep of his gun hand. "And guests."

The other Human bit his lips as he obviously thought about what his orders must be. Should he ask a superior what to do, or risk making the wrong decision here?

Lazarus had a communicative face, but she now realized that he didn't give away much of his inner commentary, to watch this other Human splay his thoughts out for everyone to see.

The man stared at Eha for a long moment, and then her. And his eyes fell, taking in her shape, her femininity, compared to the coldly alien shape of Eha Dunham.

Aileen smiled at the man and cocked her ears and whiskers as he thought.

"Very good, sir," the doorman announced after a long heartbeat. "Go right in."

He did something and Aileen heard the wooden door unlock with a thunk.

Again, Pryce led. Lazarus slipped to the side to wait, so Aileen ended up second in line.

Old house, converted perhaps to a museum at some point, before falling into private hands. The floors were hardwoods, stained deep and then scuffed and polished several times. The walls had the look of gypsum board, rather than metal or wood, and were hung with a variety of strange art. Humans, places, plants, and animals.

Grand staircase up to a second floor, with a velvet rope across the bottom, so apparently private quarters, or something. Pryce turned right anyway and entered into a lounge done in *middle-aged wealthy male.*

Aileen would have decorated differently, but she'd see Innruld chambers decorated in a similar manner. The same wooden floors, covered over now with large rugs in places. Wood paneled walls a little darker than Eha's golden stripes. Big, round table made of a deep brown wood covered over with green cloth in the center of the room, with a wetbar off to one side and chairs and end tables scattered around the walls. It was a big space, so the dozen or so Humans in here still left it feeling empty.

Aileen could identify the staff by the black they wore. Pants, shirts, aprons. Plus a level of professionalism to their faces as everyone came to a screeching halt and turned to stare at them.

At her. She was first. Pryce had stepped to one side to let everyone gape at her.

Aileen smiled and walked over to the bar. It was three and a half feet tall, comfortable for Humans and at the bottom of her neck. The woman behind it was tall and rail thin.

"I don't do alcohol," Aileen announced, as if this was the most natural thing in the world. "Do you have any lemonade?"

One beat. Two. Brain kicked in and hands started to move again.

"Right away," she said, grabbing a mug made of glass and filling it with ice.

Aileen didn't get the fetish Humans had to put ice in everything, but now was not the time to complicate the poor woman's mind.

A clear pitcher came up and the bartender poured.

"That looks divine," Eha said a moment later from just to Aileen's left. "I'll have the same."

Even bigger gawk. Mouth fallen all the way open in utter shock. Several blinks while her body was on autopilot to make a second glass.

"Whiskey sour, soft, for me," Lazarus had stepped up on her other side.

She watched him place a bill on the counter between them. It was far larger than even a private club on Yisan should charge from what he'd told her. About what he had paid for their dinner, but she presumed this was a bonus to the woman for not losing her cool.

"And you, sir?" the woman asked, whites in her eyes still a little too obvious.

"I'll have a glass of the red blend, neat," Pryce said.

Aileen took her glass with a smile and sipped it. Good. Lemon juice, simple syrup, and water. Nothing complicated. Nothing potentially poisonous.

Let the Humans drink alcohol and destroy themselves.

The gamblers had all risen as she stepped away from the bar. Because she felt like putting her stamp on things, Aileen smiled and gave them all a half-bow, like she would a dear uncle back home.

Several replied identically, but she could tell it was an automatic thing, and not planned out.

"Gentlemen, don't let me interrupt your game," she cooed at them sweetly as she moved to one of the chairs to the side and picked out a place to sit.

Human chairs, designed for people with impossible legs. She could see tasking Thadrakho with making her something that would fold up quickly and discreetly. Maybe with telescoping legs so she could sit and then elevate herself to be on a par with the Humans.

She watched Eha and the men get studied in turn.

This was going to be so exhausting, but worth it.

SEVENTEEN

EHA

THE PLACE HAD A FULL KITCHEN. Eha could tell that by the smells emanating from the door to the rear of the building. The smell of shock, surprise, and maybe a little fear also filled the room a few moments later.

Lazarus had warned her that some Humans had a psychological aversion to snakes, and would likely be triggered by her arrival, but she hadn't grasped the significance until now. Most of the men and women at the table were just shocked, but one of the men moved around to the other side of the table, immediately opposite her, eyes wide with fear and breath shallow and raspy.

Eha nodded severely to the man and moved to a space close to Aileen and coiled herself. A pillow would be nice, even a blanket folded over a few times. She wasn't in the mood to try to drape her coil comfortably across a wingback chair.

Probably, she'd end up tipping herself over if she did.

That Human settled some when she did. The others looked like they wanted to say or do something, but Lazarus and Oluchi Pryce intercepted them. Distracted them, even.

That one man continued to mutter angrily under his breath, from the way his mouth moved, but Eha was too far away to hear anything. His body language was negative enough.

She could see where Pryce had pushed the limits of his invitation, especially by apparently not warning these players what he was going to do tonight. Who he was going to bring. On the one side of the scales, it might engender some hard feelings, and these men and women all looked like they had wealth, and presumably some level of personal power.

On the other side of the coil, it would also likely disturb these men at a visceral level, at a time when high-stakes poker meant a rather large sum of money could be expected to change hands.

Eha wondered if Oluchi Pryce had already worn out his welcome, or perhaps stretched these players as far as they would go in losing money to him. Perhaps he was close to burning his standing invitation, and had decided to go out in a blaze of glory?

Would he try to get himself invited along on the next leg of Lazarus's trip? Eha supposed many would be quite interested. How much trade did these two alien women represent, when everyone at the table was a merchant of some sort, based on what Pryce had offered earlier?

She settled next to Aileen with a secret smile they shared and watched the room slowly settle down into something vaguely close what it had been earlier. She could see things well from here, and had a spare chair next to her for a Human who had perhaps tired of the game and wanted to chat.

Eha studied Oluchi Pryce as he realized that he might be tied up in a game when someone else tried to engage her in conversation. That might balance the scales a bit, giving him a distraction as well.

He nodded at her in wry acknowledgment of the changed situation and smiled just a hint.

Yes, she would make a splash. And it would put her in a position to do something about the Innruld, with folks who would be more interested in money than politics, if she was reading the faces and calculations around her correctly.

EIGHTEEN

LAZARUS

LAZARUS HAD WALKED into the building with the faintest bit of nervousness about him. Private events like this could go several ways, especially once he saw the sort of neighborhood they had entered.

Not the oldest part of the colony.

No, simply the wealthiest. Provincial, to be sure, this far away from the rest of the so-called civilized galaxy at places like Brasilia, but the men and women would be the social powers on this planet.

Lazarus wondered if Pryce had bitten off more than the man could chew.

The drink in his hand was well-made, in spite of the cold water the women had dunked the bartender into when they ordered. Pryce was playing things like he did this every day, and not just the opportunity of a lifetime for someone with the balls to run with it.

The women seated, Lazarus followed Pryce to the table. Eight men, four women. Ages roughly thirty-five to nearly dead. He and the women were the only ones with visible weapons, but he had no doubt that the staff could bring out heavy firepower if they needed, and someone was probably calling in a few favors right now to bring more folks around.

Just in case.

Lazarus got introduced to everyone, but most had remained standing. One man on the far side of the table had gone white and verged on hyperventilating, but sat now and drank hard from a highball of whiskey.

One man seemed to dominate things as Lazarus took the temperature of the table.

Eduardo Martìnez. Tall and portly, with a full head of white hair and muttonchops, dressed in a severe black suit that Lazarus might have seen in his grandfather's closet when he was young.

"Lazarus, you say?" Martìnez inquired with narrowed eyes.

"Indeed, sir," he replied. "Lazarus of Bethany, if you will. At the time, I was firmly convinced of my impending mortality, so I prayed to God for help and a sign. He offered me His Grace. It has gotten me this close to home, in the company of two of my friends."

"Just two?"

"We're scouts, as it were," he offered obliquely. "I was not sure what sort of reception I might get, just with a Churquen and a Yithadreph, let alone Qooph, Vaadwig, Kr'mari, Tarni, Ilount, and others. From here, my goal is Brasilia."

Lazarus rather enjoyed the way all those eyes got wide with whites for a second as the implications hit. Not just two aliens, but entire new multi-alien polities, perhaps?

"Brasilia?" Martìnez asked. "Are you carrying cargo?"

"We're currently on Yisan aboard the rough equivalent of a pincke, sir," Lazarus said. "That limits what I can haul back to the mothership."

Again, just dangle things out there. They didn't need to

know that it was a light starcruiser of the Rio Alliance Navy, currently understaffed. Or how desperate certain things were.

Lazarus's goal was to present so much larger than he really was, on the hopes that nobody would call his bluff. Mothership suggested something far more dangerous. And against freighters and patrol craft, he had no doubts that even Wybert could handle trouble.

"But I'm interrupting your game, ladies and gentlemen," Lazarus smiled and gestured to the poker table. "Pray, continue, and I will join my companions for a time while we watch. They had an interest in learning about Human culture."

Lazarus bowed deeply to the group and withdrew to the side. Rather than take the chair next to Eha, he flagged down a waiter.

"Could you locate a large pillow or perhaps a quilt or two for my friend to rest upon?" he smiled, watching the waiter flinch when he turned and scamper out of the room, no doubt to loot some room upstairs.

Lazarus smiled and pulled a chair up on Aileen's side, so she didn't have to deal with someone wanting to *chat*. She'd be grace itself if they did, but he also knew how much it would exhaust the woman, to put up such a front with strangers.

And everyone would want to talk to Eha, anyway, if they could work up the courage.

Lazarus noted the one man directly across the table, and the sour, angry looks that flashed this way. Should have moved himself ninety degrees, so he didn't have to watch, but Lazarus supposed he feared someone sneaking up on him.

He settled down and studied the rest of these folks, trying to identify which might prove to be allies.

He would need friends.

NINETEEN

OLUCHI

WELL, Oluchi, you've put your foot into it this time, haven't you?

But he didn't let any of that appear on his face. Or even in his fingertips.

Two hands in, and Strav Ardna had folded suddenly, rose in a huff, and stomped right out the room, not even bothering to collect his chips.

Things had fallen silent for a moment, but all these players had legacies together stretching back decades before Oluchi ever arrived in-system, so when they made no comment, he just smiled vacuously and counted his cards.

And everyone else's.

His plan had been to shim his way in when he introduced the aliens to the money people around here, so he didn't get cut out of a deal later. If nothing else, most of them would happily drop a finder's fee on him, knowing he could have split town with the group and offered to guide them to other ports he knew.

A couple of friendly nods his way right now just reinforced that notion.

Both Martìnez and Lady Leena Hernández acknowledged some debt. That would be something he could collect on later.

"If I understand things, and mind you this is all rumor and innuendo," Leena murmured quietly now, just for players at the table, "Strav has always had a terror of snakes and such."

She nodded over Oluchi's shoulder at where the two alien women sat and watched politely.

"Pryce, you were such a wicked boy for springing such a surprise on us," she continued.

Oluchi pasted a smile on his face and gave a brief nod. Most of these people paid exorbitant fees to find anything *interesting*. When you had that much money, it became like oxygen, only notable by its sudden absence.

Your greatest fear wasn't sudden poverty so much as terminal *ennui*.

Leena was a tall, rail thin scarecrow of a woman, both the daughter and widow of major shipping houses in this sector. Her two grown children ran the houses now, leaving this woman free to *pursue* her strange appetites.

He had been the flavor of the month with Leena. Even bedded her a time or two, but she hid a dark side that he hadn't really cottoned to, although he supposed there were men and women she could hire who would make it as rough as she seemed to need to get fully aroused.

That sort of boudoir brutality usually left him soft and distracted. But she could be quite interesting, once you got her out of the bedroom.

Not as much fun as Fernanda, seated on Oluchi's immediate left. Lady Flores was a matronly, grandmotherly type, to look at her, a few pounds heavier than idealized beauty, but way more fun in bed than Leena. And she enjoyed all manner of physical hobbies: hiking, camping, surfing, and skiing, that had seen her kidnap him for long weeks of actual pleasure, both in the bedroom as well as over the dinner table.

So rare to find a woman who liked to talk as much as she liked to fuck.

"Should we call a break, or continue playing?" Fernanda asked.

"Strav's always throwing a fit over something," Eduardo Martìnez said from what felt like the head of an otherwise round table. "If he decides to have a snit, we'll just leave his chips for next week."

The others grunted or nodded and play continued, but Oluchi had his concerns. Never good to burn a bridge with someone at this table. Even someone he hadn't done much business with before.

Unless it was time for him to try to join the adventurers on their journey. There shouldn't be any active warrants out for his arrest, once you got close enough to Brasilia, assuming he could get them to skip over a few places closer to Yisan.

Oluchi concentrated on his cards and his neighbors. He might need a pretty good stake, if he was going to be done with Tershuvi Port for a while.

TWENTY

EHA

SHE SUSPECTED that the long break for a communal meal was something this group didn't normally do, at least not unless they had interesting guests, but Eha was watching the Human players like a herd of galumphs tonight.

They seemed to feel it, too, as the table apparently had a strange tilt to it tonight, with Oluchi Pryce and Eduardo Martìnez seeming to win two of every four hands between them. The elder Human had depths of stability and intellect to him that the others apparently did not. It would be interesting to determine what made him such a formidable player.

And avoid becoming his prey.

A waiter had entered and waited close by the table until a hand was completed, and then stepped up and whispered in Martìnez's ear. The man nodded, the waiter vanished, and he turned his magnanimous gaze on the players, before extending it to the room.

"I believe the buffet is ready," he said. "I propose a longer break than normal. What say you?"

General assent. Eha didn't think many of the others were

able to concentrate on their cards anyway, to their own detriment. Certainly, faces kept drifting over to study her when they should have been on their own cards.

She rose from her coil now as the Humans did. Beside her, Aileen slipped off the chair and stretched. It had been roughly an hour since the players had recovered from the one Human stomping out angrily and departing without a word.

The older Human approached in a manner Eha could only classify as gingerly. Slow, measured steps but without any speed or emphasis behind them. Both Lazarus and Oluchi Pryce moved faster under normal circumstances. Both of them were off to one side like a receiving line, but the other man stepped to her, rather than the men.

"Eduardo Martìnez," he said as he got close enough to offer her a hand.

Eha still found the Human custom bizarre, offering your right hand as indication that there wasn't a weapon in it, but she also understood that it was the courteous way to establish yourself as equals, without the need to measure the depth of a formal bow to a relative stranger.

"Eha Dunham," she replied. "Churquen Ambassador."

Human flesh was strange. Scaleless. Furless. Normally a little less moist than this, from the times she had done the same with Lazarus in practice. She had steeled herself for the man potentially gripping and squeezing in an attempt at dominance, but his grip was perfunctory. He released and introduced himself to Aileen.

There, there was at least fur to distract him, because she could see in his eyes the strangeness of her scales.

Good, let us establish a working relationship of equals as strangers, Eduardo Martìnez.

Quickly, the others did the same. Eha memorized the names and faces, but of the men, only Eduardo seemed interesting, and two of the women, both of whom paused to kiss Oluchi Pryce on both cheeks warmly, before doing the same with Lazarus. She and Aileen got simple handshakes as well, although both Leena Hernández and Fernanda Flores had the look that they might have welcomed brushing faces with fur or scales.

Humans grinned with teeth, but Eha just smiled back at them, unwilling to show her sharper fangs.

Eduardo Martìnez led the group into a room across the building, which had been set up for communal dining. The staff had set out a series of tables against the far wall next to another wetbar and put out food in large troughs with heating elements.

Eha breathed a sigh of relief. Communal generally meant mild, especially as older Humans frequently didn't have the digestive tolerance that younger ones did. Or maybe anything left to prove. This group looked like the latter.

The funniest thing that she kept behind a façade of reserve was establishing precedence in eating. Eha could tell that the group themselves, without any outsiders, would fall into a rough pecking order that saw Eduardo at the front, with the others in declining relevance, but Oluchi had thrown everything awry.

As had Aileen, being so much shorter than the others. Someone had apparently run out and located enough wood to build a small walkway next to the table in front of the food, so a Yithadreph didn't have to stand on her toes when inspecting the offerings.

Nobody had asked about food sensitivities, but Oluchi gave her a nod that suggested he might have warned the staff to go easy, even before arriving.

That Human liked his surprises, apparently. Something else to keep in mind.

"As we are merely guests tonight, it would never do to impose on our hosts, sir," Lazarus stepped up and bowed politely to Eduardo, gesturing for the man to precede them. "Please, we will need a moment as I explain the dishes to the others."

And it made a fast way for the others to get at the food while it was fresh, and see if anybody avoided anything.

The Humans gave way and ate, some gorging and others taking a few choice bits. The food seemed heavy on seafood dishes, with shrimp in a sauced pasta, fish cuts wrapped up and deep fried or baked. Various vegetable side dishes. Bread, which had been an interesting discovery, as the Human wheat flour gave it a different taste and amazing rise over the kinds they got back home.

There was more food than this group would eat in a day, but she supposed the staff prepared an overabundance and ate the leftovers, or something. Eha chose to be dainty tonight, sampling from several of the troughs in the same pattern as Lazarus had, with him giving both of them a quiet, running commentary on ingredients and occasionally asking one of the helpers additional questions.

They ate at another table that appeared to be two rectangles pushed together under a cloth. There were two such in here, and the groups divided into those sitting close enough to engage in conversation, and those on the far side of the other where they could watch.

Again, the dynamics had Eduardo Martìnez on her immediate left, with Oluchi beyond him and Aileen on her right, with Lazarus beyond that. Good, Aileen could have some degree of privacy, and she and Lazarus could handle questions, although the two women, Leena and Fernanda, had had their own battle, with Leena ending up around the same corner from Lazarus and Fernanda across from him.

She had little doubt what those two were about. Some looks transcended species.

"Did I understand you correctly, Mistress Dunham?" Eduardo asked. "Churquen Ambassador?"

"That is correct," she replied, only taking small bites of things.

She had already eaten enough today, but Lazarus had explained how meals tended to be as much social event as anything.

"Is Churquen a world or a species?" he asked the obvious follow-up she had dangled in front of him.

"Species," she smiled with her eyes. "Aileen is a Yithadreph. I'm originally from Gowook, and most recently have been working on Dormell and Zhoonarrim. Those are planets."

Nice to also dangle out there that she came from a rather large place. She didn't say hundreds of worlds, but perhaps implied it by casually mentioning just three.

How bad do you want to trade with us, Human?

"And what will those coordinates cost us?" he smiled primly. "I presume that Lazarus's purpose in going to Brasilia is to establish diplomatic ties with the Rio Alliance, but we're outside of that space. And those rules."

The others made similar noises of agreement.

Eha had never really processed that a planet could exist on its own, without formal ties to a larger organization, but the Innruld controlled everything ruthlessly. Even more ruthlessly than she had previously imagined, since no colonies could be built except where the Innruld chose, with overlords and the bureaucratic infrastructure already in place.

That was what made the Humans and their allies so dangerous.

Freedom from oversight.

Worlds might choose to join the Rio Alliance, and they might not. Same with Westphalia, although many of the worlds they controlled now had not been theirs originally.

"There are complications," Eha replied, turning to stare at the Human directly. "I'm given to understand that a Human civil war rages in this sector of the galaxy. We would prefer that it not embroil us as well."

Eduardo nodded at that, not accepting that as a rejection, so much as tabling it as an opening bid and answer, part of a much longer and potentially profitable conversation.

A relationship.

How bad do you want to trade with us, Human?

"How many species are there in your sectors?" Fernanda asked.

She had the look of an adventurer about her, compared to Leena.

Lazarus had suggested that very pale skin on a Human usually indicated someone who was rarely out in the sun, with the skin darkening. Eha also understood that most of the Humans at the table represented an ethnic variance from what she knew, being already darker than Lazarus or Oluchi and tending towards a reddish-brown skin tone and black hair. Fernanda had wrinkles around her eyes and spots on her skin suggesting advanced age, but a youthful vitality about her anyway.

"Many," Eha turned to her and smiled. "Living in a more peaceful existence over a fairly compact region of space."

As in, you can't just start looking and hope to find us randomly. If nothing else, the nebula between us will slow you down for decades, without better maps than Lazarus had had available.

"But you are here for trade?" Eduardo asked, drawing an underline on the only thing that interested him.

"Actually, technically we are here to return Lazarus to his home," Aileen spoke up. "The law makes it incumbent on a ship when they rescue a marooned sailor. Aceanx just wasn't acceptable as a destination, for reasons that should be obvious."

Eha liked the way the Yithadreph woman smiled at everyone, reminding them that the two of them represented an interstellar nation of laws, and not just a potential feeding frenzy of commerce to be had.

Eha had originally had her doubts about bringing Aileen Enjehn along, but every single hour, she became better convinced that Lazarus had been right to do so. None of the other crew had the calmness around strangers, and the intellectual curiosity to handle this mission.

"So Rio will get all the trade?" Eduardo continued to probe.

"Certainly not, sir," Eha smiled at him. "However, we also don't need Human pirates in our space, and I did not notice any significant military or police forces in this system that could be called upon to protect commerce. And well-armed merchantmen might present their own problems, necessitating that our own vessels be capable of dealing with them if they turn out to be wolves in sheep's clothing."

Eduardo seemed to take that at face value. Or was willing to be deflected. These men and women might not be pirates themselves, but they also chose to live in a place outside the Rio Alliance and those laws. Most probably had a host of smugglers in their employ, as well as a few pirates, under some other legal and social classification.

Lazarus had been an encyclopedia of information, once Eha had decided to empty his brain about the Rio Alliance and places like Yisan. She certainly was far better prepared for this dinner than anyone else might have been.

Instead of pursuing things, Eha got the others to talk about themselves, their hobbies, and their trade houses. Relationships into Rio space or Westphalia. Useful things she might learn or need, while making it clear that she would keep them all in mind favorably when it came time to establish trade.

To deal.

Eha could see the need to funnel some goods through here, if only because that would let her engage with a wider swath of Humans than just the Rio Alliance. Yisan wasn't directly on the route to Innruld space, but it wasn't that far out of the way, either.

Especially if she could lay her hands on Human star drives.

That would break open the entire galaxy when the Humans broke the Innruld for her.

TWENTY-ONE

LAZARUS

LAZARUS WAS EXHAUSTED, but didn't dare show it. Even in the vehicle leaving the poker event to return to the port, he still had an audience in Oluchi Pryce. Still, the man had been helpful, above and beyond anything Lazarus had expected of bringing the women to Yisan.

They had gotten a first class introduction to Human society, and made enough contacts here that he could see a significant amount of trade eventually flowing this way.

Would that make Yisan eventually turn into its own place? Right now, it was outside of Rio Alliance space and control, and provided enough of a pressure valve that significant trade could pass through here on the way to Westphalia, as long as everyone behaved.

Innruld space would suddenly cast Yisan and a few others like it into middlemen geographically, instead of just socially. Was he in the process of forcing a third stellar nation to be born?

Interesting, in and of itself, but what would that mean to the Rio Alliance, to potentially have a new neighbor between them and new allies? Lazarus wasn't sure, but he also didn't think it would be something solved in his lifetime, unless things went terribly awry one way or the other.

Ajax couldn't break Westphalia, but the design might make them behave better. As might adding dozens of new species. None of those groups were big enough to threaten Human domination anywhere, at least not in the short term, but it opened up options if he threw open the floodgates.

How did he want to go down in the history books? Up until now, Lazarus had never expected to be more than a random footnote, forgotten for the most part. Now he would be the subject of books, movies, and slander.

Pryce was studying him closely as the car rolled along. Far more than the occasional looks the women were getting.

Lazarus decided to confront the situation head on. He'd been on the planet for all of a day at this point, and could easily depart tomorrow, after sleeping enough to feel safe taking off. Aileen looked even more ragged, but she'd been keeping up her social persona for too long with too many people to suit her.

"What's your game, Pryce?" Lazarus asked.

"Oluchi," he said quietly.

They were literally touching shoulders in the back of the car.

"Oluchi," Lazarus accepted.

"You're big," Oluchi said. "All of this is just the tip of some iceberg. And it goes deeper than just two alien women hauling you to Brasilia to meet with big shots. I've played enough poker against top-notch players in my time to recognize that."

"And?" Lazarus prompted him.

"And I want a cut of that," Oluchi said. "I want in on the action. I've already showed you that I can get you into the room with a bunch of people who might not have given you the time of day. And keep them interested enough to talk, but deflected enough to keep it polite."

"And the one man who left early?" Lazarus played a hunch. "Ardna? What's your history with him?"

He watched the man, but Oluchi Pryce had a face that gave nothing away. After a moment, the gambler relaxed, perhaps relented, and Lazarus saw the first emotions in those eyes he'd seen all day.

Whether or not they were honest was a different story. Lazarus wasn't a poker player, but he'd known enough of them in his time to appreciate that they were all actors.

"Strav Ardna might have lost a considerable sum of money to me over the last few evenings like tonight," Oluchi's face screwed up sideways into a partial grin. "Enough that even someone like that would notice the amounts. Plus, he's always thought of himself as a ladies man, and both Leena and Fernanda sort of iced him out in favor of the new kid."

"So jealousy, across a wide swath of issues?" Eha spoke up. "Were you aware that he would be utterly terrified of Churquen?"

Oluchi turned to her and Lazarus saw some of the man's mask spall off pieces, showing the person behind it. Not much, but not the cold, ruthless purveyor of *bonhomie* that had sat at the table and made a small fortune tonight.

Not just him, anyway.

"That was as much a surprise to me as it was to you," Pryce admitted. "I had planned to use you to distract everyone, which you did, and to deflect his pique away from me, because I didn't figure I'd be invited back again after pulling a stunt like this."

"Blaze of glory?" Lazarus asked.

"*Exit stage left, pursued by a bear,*" Oluchi grinned.

"Never make a mundane entrance or a forgettable departure."

"So now what?" Lazarus circled him back to the key topic.

"So you're lifting off soon," Oluchi said. "That much is obvious from the way the three of you are sitting right now. You came to Yisan to learn some things, found them whatever they are, and are bouncing out of here for points deeper into the Alliance. Maybe tonight. Probably tomorrow. If I don't move right now, you'll be gone and I'll be on my own."

"And?" Lazarus let his voice convey a chill now.

"And I don't want to overplay my hand and say you need me, because you don't for what you have planned, Lazarus of Bethany who has been raised from the dead," Oluchi turned more serious now. "But you will need someone like me, because this is bigger than just the Rio Alliance government. Am I right?"

The latter addressed to Eha. Lazarus turned to her now.

Oluchi had guessed right about one thing. Lazarus had never lived by his wits on the streets. He was an expert on bureaucratic warfare in the halls of the military and how to properly fawn over government officials with purse strings in their hands. He could fake some savvy, but Oluchi Pryce exuded it like an expensive cologne.

"It has the potential, Oluchi Pryce," Eha replied, her voice taking on a much deeper and more serious timbre now than he could remember before. "Why are you the man to explore it?"

Lazarus caught the stutter as the man bit back the first pithy reply that wanted to emerge. Watched him chew over the words more carefully while studying the three of them.

Finally, a thumb came up to indicate Lazarus, but the eyes stayed on Eha.

"That's his one weakness, if he has any," Oluchi said in a voice so deadly serious that Lazarus thought an imposter had taken over the man's body. "He screams military, but he was marooned in your space."

Lazarus blinked in unconscious surprise that this stranger had been able to place him so well. Had any of the others, or was it something special about this gambler?

"That makes him a Rio Alliance explorer," Oluchi was continuing. "Probably an officer off doing things nobody was supposed to know about when he had a problem and you rescued him. You, Eha Dunham, want more trade and communication than the Rio government might be willing to allow, so you've hedged your bets with Martìnez and the others here, but you're about to drop into the maw at Brasilia and then all of Human space explodes. Close?"

Lazarus found he had stopped breathing. Eha and Aileen maybe, as well. Oluchi watched all of them, smiled, and leaned back.

"Close enough," he said, back to the happy-go-lucky gambler who'd sat down at their table in a tea room and introduced himself.

Nobody spoke for a few moments.

"I've folded a full house on the fifth card," he offered, voice returning to serious for a moment. Almost deadly. "Knowing that the man across the table is sitting on four queens just by the way he's breathing. Lazarus, you might be the big king shit on the bridge of a warship, but you're an open book. I want to be her middleman to the trade houses. One of them, anyway. Even a slice of a percentage is likely to turn into a swimming pool full of coins I could swim in, like the ancient cartoons."

Lazarus didn't have words. He'd never met a clinical psychologist who was a mind reader as well. Certainly never expected one to dress so snappily.

He turned to Eha. She'd been working the room with promises of trade. Lazarus understood that *Ajax* and friends were what she would need to knock the overlord Innruld off their perch, but without Human trade, the species over there were all galumphs just waiting for the butcher to come round. They would need Human tech, Human trade, Human help outside of official channels.

Westphalia would never go for it, but the Rio Alliance might be getting maneuvered into a position where they had to help with open hands, because trying to close a fist would squish all the mud between their fingers.

"You're close, Oluchi," Eha said. "But there are things you don't know, and probably can't read on any of us well enough yet. There are secrets yet, because those trade caravans must wait for a time."

"You're fighting your own war," he said flatly.

Whether it was a guess, or the man had learned Churquen physiology as well in the last twelve hours.

"It's much worse than that," Aileen spoke up now.

Lazarus had caught the glance the two women shared. The subtle nod Eha gave Aileen before she spoke. Held his breath.

The Yithadreph loadmaster leaned forward enough to look around Lazarus. Oluchi was all eyes now.

"We're after revolution."

TWENTY-TWO
LAZARUS

THE REST of the ride had been pretty much in silence, which had suited Lazarus. Oluchi was obviously still digesting things. Lazarus was tired. Aileen and Eha were in silent communication that he really wasn't offended to miss.

They were close to the port now, winding through some of the older, smaller streets with tall warehouses on all sides.

The vehicle slowed suddenly. Jammed on the brakes hard enough that Eha was nearly knocked off her coil.

"What?"

Lazarus started to turn to see what the problem was, when another vehicle suddenly appeared from an alley and stopped right behind them, blocking this one from moving.

Figures on foot surrounded the limo they were riding in. Guns were pointed inward.

Lots of guns.

Lazarus didn't figure the metalwork of the vehicle would do much to stop them.

"Oh, crap," Oluchi muttered with such vehemence that Lazarus presumed they probably weren't friends of his.

A fist rapped on the window. Made it clear that they

could open the door, or have it opened for them.

Oluchi turned to him with honest fear in his eyes, like maybe he'd stayed in on a hand he should have folded earlier.

"What do we do?" he breathed.

"Open it," Eha ordered. "There's not much we can do, and they won't wait long before asking harder."

Lazarus considered drawing his pistol, but that would just get them all killed right now, assuming that wasn't already somebody's plan. Westphalians?

No, this did not feel like a bunch of random spacers deciding to cause trouble. Things like that got you evicted, even in a place like Yisan, with instructions to never return.

No ship's crew would push their luck that hard on the ground.

Oluchi cycled the lock and a man outside pulled the door open, kneeling down with a sub-machinegun pointed into the back and a crude smile on his face.

"Pistols first, if you want to live," he snarled in a rough tone. "Not asking twice and I'll kill you if you give me any grief. Savvy?"

Oluchi glanced back and Lazarus nodded. It was a trap, but hopefully somebody just wanted to talk. There wasn't anything any of them could do right now.

The gambler gingerly reached down and slid his pistol out and held it for the stranger to take and hand off to one of the others. Lazarus went next while the other two sat perfectly still, probably watching the others around them.

The glass was clear enough that someone standing close with a barrel resting on the outside could see in. There were at least six men in that category.

Aileen passed her Manticore over, and then Eha's went.

"Good," the man said in a brighter voice, still sounding like a ballpeen hammer trying to drive a sheared-off nail deep enough to ignore. "Bodies next and don't get stupid, right?"

He rose and stepped back, that one barrel never wavering for an instant, not that Lazarus figured he could do anything right now but die stupidly.

Oluchi climbed out of the vehicle and was manhandled over to the truck, hands on the metal and feet spread like he was being arrested.

None of the men had badges, but the frisking was expert, as Lazarus emerged next and got the same treatment. Someone left their uniforms at home?

Aileen popping out brought a round of mutters from the dozen men around him. They weren't all dressed alike in anything like uniforms or combat attire, but they all had the look of rough men from the docks.

The kinds you crossed to a different street to avoid if you saw them in port.

"What's this?" the man frisking her snarled.

"That's my tail, you dork," Aileen snapped at him. "Keep your hands to yourself."

Lazarus feared things were going to get ugly, but the man stepped back with a satisfied nod.

Eha nearly caused the men to lose it.

Cries of shock and fear emerged from the crowd around them, even as they kept guns centered. At least Lazarus had been able to turn and watch.

Eha looked like the Empress of the Universe as she slithered out and stared at the man who seemed to be in charge.

This was exactly the opposite of the mongoose and the cobra, whatever that was. The man wasn't a rabbit, but he turned white around the edges.

"You, too, princess," he managed in a gruff tone.

Eha stretched on her coil and rotated enough to place her hands on the side of the vehicle.

"You like snakes?" she murmured as the man stepped

close, too tough to admit intimidation, but at least more nervous than the others.

Gloved hands ran down her sides and patted pockets, the man trying not to touch her tail with his legs. When he was done, she turned and smiled at him.

"You missed one," Eha offered, pointing at a pocket where a Human woman would have had breasts.

Aileen hadn't been groped, tail notwithstanding.

The man hesitated.

"Go on, then," their leader snapped.

Lazarus was sure Eha leaned into the man's hand as he reached out to pat her chest. Must have learned that trick from Aileen, because he couldn't remember ever telling her something that would cause her to do that with Humans.

The man shivered, but did his job and then nodded to the other. Their Chief.

Lazarus thought of the man as a Chief Petty Officer, a non-comm in charge of enlisted men. This group had that feel to it. Marines out causing unofficial trouble.

"Right," the CPO in charge said. "My orders were to pick up the two women and take them to the boss. You lot get back in the car and return to your ship or you'll get hurt right now."

Oluchi started to say something and one of the others on this shore party grabbed him by the collar with a hard jerk.

"I'd like that," the CPO continued. "You get stupid and me'n'th'boys will see you put. Get me?"

He was staring at Lazarus now, daring something.

Six on one, unarmed when you had guns? Not my day.

Lazarus nodded briefly to the CPO, admitting defeat.

Live to fight another day.

He grabbed Oluchi and propelled him into the car before the local did anything else stupid.

If they made the mistake of letting him get to his ship, he

could always escape into space, even if something happened to Aileen and Eha.

And if those two were hurt, he would find the people who did it and bring *Ajax* back here. Kirov's Lance could punch a hole in an atmosphere. The beam would attenuate a little, but only enough to annihilate an entire house and most of the yard from orbit to a depth of a few feet.

Or maybe turn someone's yacht into a puddle of smoking metal. With you aboard.

He didn't let any of that into his eyes, because he needed to stay alive.

Addison might not stop at just killing everyone responsible, if something happened to Eha. He might burn the whole city to the ground, and Lazarus just might help at that point.

Before Oluchi could speak, Lazarus climbed in and the CPO slammed the door shut. A moment later, the car began to move again.

"I'm going to need your help," Lazarus explained in a voice that felt like death as he looked back. "Whether you like it or not."

Behind them, the two women were being hustled into a van.

"Oh, I'm already in, whatever it is," Oluchi's anger almost matched Lazarus now. "I recognized that man, although he might not realize it."

"Oh?"

"He works for Ardna," Oluchi said.

Lazarus nodded. He might not stop Addison at just destroying Tershuvi, if anything happened to Eha.

It might be time to end Yisan as a pirate haven.

Maybe as an inhabited planet.

Ajax could handle that.

TWENTY-THREE
OLUCHI

OUT OF THE FRYING PAN, into the fire. Oluchi's mom had said that about her son more than once, as he always tried to fast-talk his way out of trouble, instead of just accepting responsibility.

Thirty years later, he still didn't do it all that often, but this was different. This was a couple of innocent strangers that were going to catch a ration of his shit for nothing they did but be born and be in the same room as him. At this point, it really didn't matter that they also might be his meal ticket.

They hadn't asked for the problems of Oluchi Pryce and his wandering dick. Ardna already hated him for giving both Leena and Fernanda someone more interesting to play with in bed or across the dinner table. Oluchi had seen the raw terror in the man's eyes seeing Eha Dunham for the first time.

Nearly pissed himself in fear. With most people, that was a useful bit of knowledge. He should have known that Strav Ardna would over-react on this one. Should have been expecting trouble on the way back, since the man had gotten a several hour head start on whatever grief he had in mind.

"We're going to need guns," Oluchi turned to the other man in the back of the limo.

"Oh, I got guns," Lazarus said in a calm, deadly, off-hand manner than froze the blood in Oluchi's veins.

The stranger suddenly sounded just like a Rio Alliance naval officer, standing on his deck and getting ready to unleash a serious ass-whooping on someone.

Did the aliens have a warship out there? Something big enough and mean enough to come down here and blow shit to Kingdom Come?

If he was looking at the apocalypse descending, Oluchi really wanted to make sure he was on the right side. The other tycoons would be miffed, but not nearly as rageful as the eyes of this redheaded stranger.

Terrible things were coming.

"What do you need?" Oluchi asked.

He could find anything. That was his super power.

You want it? I know a guy.

"Can you use a gun?" Lazarus asked, those sharp, green eyes boring in now. "And I mean kill someone because he's in your way, or stepped out of the wrong door, or you don't like the cut of his suit? That's where this is going."

Oluchi shivered in spite of himself. You had to be hard and dangerous to make a living as a gambler. Sometimes, charming the ladies came with the gig. They required even more effort.

Lazarus looked like a man about to kill everyone he met for the next twelve hours. Oluchi had known a few of those over the years. Most of them had been ex-soldiers who couldn't handle civilian life, and had gravitated to a life of brutality.

It never ended well.

Lazarus of Bethany might just kick in the door and shoot everyone in the room, from the raw anger in his eyes.

"I can," Oluchi said simply.

No braggadocio. No hype.

Lazarus was clearly past any sort of showing off. Those two were just a pair of alien women that Oluchi knew. They were Lazarus's friends. This had suddenly turned into the point in the movie where the hero rounded up his posse and went to rescue the princess.

After killing everybody in the tower first.

Oluchi took a deep breath and gulped past a throat that wanted to choke.

"I know a guy," he offered.

Lazarus's smile turned colder than the hell of Oluchi's youth, back when religion still offered some greater purpose than pleasure.

"I need information," Lazarus said instead. "If that's Ardna, where is he and where are Aileen and Eha going right now?"

Oluchi pulled his comm and selected a contact number in town. Smart gamblers make friends and offer favors for cheap, so they can call things in later.

Like now.

"Hey, Oluchi," a man's deep, gruff voice came on the line. Xiuying Bălan. "How's the gigolo business?"

Oluchi kept the snarl to himself.

"Good enough," he replied. "Got a bigger problem tonight."

"Those alien chicks end up being too kinky for even you?" Xiuying asked with a crude laugh. "I might be willing to give them a go."

"Somebody just kidnapped them out of the back of my

limo at gunpoint, Xiuying," Oluchi said quietly. "Pretty sure I know who's behind it. You doing anything tonight?"

"I was working, but they can cover for me," the man's voice turned to a cold, steel blade. "Or hire a replacement. Ardna?"

"Khan was there with a bunch of his friends," Oluchi said. "Don't figure he's dumb enough to do something like this on his own."

"Where do you want me?" Xiuying asked.

"We're headed to the port," Oluchi said. He turned to Lazarus. "At the ship?"

Lazarus nodded.

"Dock fifty-three," the Rio Alliance officer said quietly.

"Dock fifty-three, Xiuying," Oluchi said. "Then I need to make some calls and see where he took them."

"Ten minutes," Xiuying said. "No, make it twenty. Need to swing by the apartment for some things first."

"Thanks, Xiuying," Oluchi said.

"No, thank you for thinking of me," Xiuying replied, cutting the signal.

"That's one," Oluchi said to Lazarus.

"Dangerous?"

"Head bouncer in one of the rougher joints on the strip," Oluchi offered. "Owes me some favors, and really hates Strav Ardna and his men for reasons best left unsaid right now."

"You can't make me any more of an accessory to murder and mayhem than tonight's going to be, Oluchi Pryce," Lazarus sneered. "You do understand that I'm not playing even remotely nice now, right? There will be blood before this is over."

Oluchi nodded back at the man. It was like he was sitting with a complete stranger now, and not the guy he'd been drinking, eating, and chatting with for most of the last ten hours.

This was who Lazarus of Bethany used to be. He and Xiuying would see eye to eye on a lot of things, at least metaphorically. Lazarus was too tall, and Xiuying too short, but yeah, murder and mayhem.

Is the brass ring worth it, Oluchi?

TWENTY-FOUR

EHA

EHA KEPT herself calm as these Humans hustled her and Aileen into a boxy ground transport, surrounding them with guns at all times. Orders were gruff monosyllables, but they didn't feel like they were intent on killing her and dumping her body on the side of the road.

Addison might never stop hunting these men if that happened. While the thought warmed her, she'd prefer talking him out of doing something personally, from the deck of *Ajax*.

Safe.

They rode in tense silence as the vehicle careened around corners and drove right out at the limits of safety. At least the windows were glass, so she could see when they headed away from the port city of Tershuvi and out towards the shore of that immense, hostile ocean that covered so much of this stupid planet.

Churquen didn't swim worth a damn. Not like Yithadreph, who were born in water. She wondered if someone had managed to read her mind and understood how much terror she would have on open water, but these

Humans were just goons. They weren't good enough actors or professional enough thugs to refrain from saying something like that right now, even if just to taunt her.

Aileen seemed to sense it, though. A hand reached out and took hers, squeezing it just enough. Eha tried to draw a breath deeper into her lungs and let calmness reach all the way to the sharp tip of her tail.

The vehicle was caught in something of a traffic jam, but the driver kept largely to his lane and followed everyone. It was the middle of the night, so she wondered if the vehicles were fishers getting ready to head out, or folks from the coast that had gone into the city for the evening, and were returning home now.

She kept her mouth tightly shut and studied the terrain. She remembered low mountains both north and south of here, but this area had appeared to be a broad river valley draining into a bay.

There were lights down there when she looked. A small city, perhaps four or five thousand people, with low, small houses clustered together mostly on the left side of the bay, with several roads running like arterials from the waterfront itself.

They followed the traffic down through the town and to the marina itself, only turning off at the end and going down a side street where many of the others ended up in a massive parking lot.

Endless rows of vehicles, just parked and waiting for the owner to return. That brought home to Eha the relative wealth of the Humans, that everyone might own a private ground vehicle for personal transportation, and just leave it someplace while they were at work.

On a station, you had tubes and slidewalks. On most planets there were well-funded mass transit systems, buses and trains to take you where you needed to be.

Of course, upon comparison, that also made it nearly impossible to do something in private on an Innruld world. You couldn't just pop into your personal vehicle, where nobody else might be able to follow you.

Huh.

She had never really appreciated how ease it must have been for the authorities to monitor dissidents and trouble-makers, back on Dormell or the Station. What if everyone could drive privately somewhere? Where an extra vehicle showing up to drop someone off might draw attention, rather than the regular bus swinging by.

She needed to start a social and economic revolution, and not just a political one.

What other useful things could she glean from the Humans?

The van came to a stop outside a fence. The punk in charge opened the sliding door and stepped out.

"You lot next," he gestured at her and Aileen.

They were already surrounded.

Aileen went first, hopping carefully down. Eha took extra time, not wanting to scare one of these hard men into doing something rash. There were warehouses around them, but across the street from where the van had parked.

The man confirmed her fears when he stepped to the gate, keyed a combination in, and opened it.

Beyond, there was a boat. Could you still call it a yacht, if it floated on water, rather than flew between stars?

Enormous. Bigger than the pincke Lazarus had flown them here aboard.

The man turned to her.

"No funny business now," he snapped and then started walking down a structure made of what Eha assumed were wooden poles stuck into the ground, with a walkway hung across them.

Wood? She could smell the rot from here. See places where some boards had previously failed and been replaced, with reddish wood slowly bleaching and decaying down to white.

They walked on something like this?

But Humans could swim. Falling in if a board broke was a matter of embarrassment, not potential death.

Aileen's hand found hers when she stopped moving, and tugged ever so lightly to get Eha in motion again. Yithadreph swam as well. Aileen's touch had a promise of safety, so Eha began to slither again, heading slowly and carefully down to a place where someone had been so insane as to float a pleasure yacht on the surface of a moving sea.

And she was surrounded by men with guns.

TWENTY-FIVE

LAZARUS

WITHOUT MUCH CHOICE in the matter, Lazarus opened the sealed hatch and ushered Oluchi Pryce into the pincke. He wasn't about to key the man into any of the systems, but Pryce had the look of a man that knew his way around security systems anyway.

Probably sneaking into a lady's boudoir for the occasional midnight assignation.

There had been more calls by Pryce. None of the rest had been recruiting, but the man looking for information. Calling in favors and offering offhand threats to people to provide information.

Blackmail was such an ugly term, but it calmed Lazarus to see the other man obviously reaching out with his own anger and tapping into the underbelly of Yisan to find out what had happened.

All that paused as Lazarus led the man back to the arms locker he had installed on this little ship before he left *Ajax*. Another code to open the lock, and Lazarus pulled the door open.

He grabbed a pistol and slid it into his holster before taking the next and holding it out to the gambler.

"That's an Ares," Oluchi said with some surprise.

"You're right," Lazarus said, reaching in and grabbing a larger holster for it. "Swap out your holster for the bigger one."

"Manticore's not good enough?" Pryce asked.

"If I have to shoot someone, I want him dead," Lazarus ground the words out like glass shards. "I'm not even taking a stunner."

Pryce gulped again and began undoing his belt.

Lazarus had assumed the man was something of a dandy, but the look in Pryce's eyes right now showed a change coming over the gambler.

We're past asking nice, son.

Oluchi nodded, took the new holster, and got everything situated just so, including the heaviest handheld blaster the Rio Navy issued.

"Here," Lazarus said as he pulled an armored vest down from the top shelf and handed it to the man, before taking one for himself and slipping off his jacket.

Both men got dressed, Pryce keeping the opera cape and Lazarus leaving his jacket open in the front.

"You want a rifle?" he asked.

"Never shot one," Oluchi replied, suggesting that maybe he knew which end of the smaller blaster went bang.

Lazarus grabbed down a blaster rifle, checked the charge, and slung it over his shoulder before closing up the locker again and heading to the cockpit.

"Now what?" Oluchi asked as Lazarus checked all the diagnostics on his boards.

Fuel, life support, systems; everything was green. It had been a short trip and he'd done a full maintenance pass on it before he left as an excuse to train Aileen on the vessel.

You hurt my loadmaster, whoever you are, and there won't be identifiable pieces of a body to bury. You hurt Eha and Addison might destroy your planet.

But he kept that inside. Kept his jaw clenched tight.

Oluchi had asked a question. He looked up at the man.

"We sit," Lazarus said. "Hopefully your friend arrives and knows what to do. Hopefully one of your other friends has the information I need. Otherwise, in twenty-six hours I lift off and go get help myself."

Oluchi shivered again, like he could subconsciously already see *Ajax* in orbit, firing Kirov's Lance into the ground at targets identified by having not already been annihilated.

Hopefully, it wouldn't come to that.

Yisan was supposed to be something of a pirate haven, but that meant that it was run by a powerful oligopoly that didn't like paying Rio Alliance taxes or dealing with rules and laws that would cramp their trading. This was still supposed to be a well-run port planet, with rules and understandings.

Lazarus didn't think that the rest of those tycoons at the poker table would get their backs up on the topic, except where maybe Ardna might steal a march on them by getting trade information that they didn't have.

It wouldn't be personal with them. Just money.

It was always that way with the incredibly wealthy. As long as they had their swindles, their games, and their mansions, they didn't trouble themselves all that much with what other tycoons did, as long as nobody crossed lines.

That two random strangers might have gotten into trouble…

Lazarus nearly jumped out of his seat when his own comm beeped.

He didn't recognize the incoming code, but took a moment to put his voice back into something close to Human before he keyed the line open.

"Lazarus," he growled.

"This is Eduardo Martìnez," the man replied. "I've just gotten off the line with Fernanda Flores, and she tells me that you believe Strav has kidnapped your two lady friends. Is that true?"

"It is," Lazarus replied bluntly, amazed that the man had found him, but he supposed a lot of favors were being offered and cashed tonight.

Oluchi's blackmail must go deeper than Lazarus had imagined. And the man was using it like a scalpel.

"What are you going to do, Lazarus?" Eduardo asked.

He had been a complete gentleman all evening. The others had been polite, but only Eduardo and Fernanda had been friendly, and Flores's ulterior motives weren't limited to trade missions."

"Once I find out where they are, I'm going to get Aileen and Eha back, Eduardo," Lazarus said in a voice that offered no emotional content whatsoever.

"I see," Eduardo said after a brief pause. "Let me make some calls."

"Thank you, Eduardo," Lazarus said and then the line went cold.

"And?" Oluchi asked.

"You've rattled a lot of cages tonight, Oluchi," Lazarus said, offering up his first smile in a while, thin and cold as it might be. "Flores and Eduardo Martìnez are apparently on our side and offering assistance. What strings should I expect?"

"If it's Fernanda, probably none from you, unless you felt like a few tumbles with an older woman who knows what she's about, is rather fun in bed, and will even cook you a pretty good breakfast in the morning," he smiled. "Leena's a bit more mercenary in those things, but Fernanda's almost someone I would consider a friend."

Lazarus checked the clock on the console.

"When's your friend arriving?" he asked.

Oluchi glanced at his watch.

"Any time now."

Lazarus nodded. A figure walking across the gravel was visible, growing closer. Male. Short and broad. Large duffel bag slung over one shoulder.

"That's him," Oluchi said, leaning forward to check. "Xiuying Bălan."

"What's his story?" Lazarus asked.

"I find things for people," Oluchi shrugged in that offhand way that suggested nobody was probably better at it on this planet. "Found him a few things. Got him a better job at a different bar than the hellhole he'd been working. Introduced him to a few women. Probably as good a friend as I have on this planet."

"No women in your life who count?" Lazarus decided to pry. The man seemed a little more open than he had been before.

"Dockside girls are generally looking for Prince Charming to take them away from all this," Oluchi scowled. "Rich ladies on the hill usually have different wants and needs. Depending on who you ask, I might have a rep here as a gigolo, but you'd be amazed how few men take the time to listen to a woman when she wants to talk, or take care of her needs before your own. You can get a lot of mileage out of simple courtesy."

"So Fernanda calling Eduardo and demanding he get involved?" Lazarus asked.

"Not what I asked her, but I could see her drawing her own conclusions," Oluchi said. "Eduardo might be the only one at that table tonight smarter than Fernanda, for pure ability to think. The others mostly inherited enormous wealth and the infrastructure to keep it intact."

"So we should trust them?" Lazarus pressed.

This was the key point.

He already had one tycoon playing fast and loose. The last thing he needed was to get into the middle of a pissing match between folks with that kind of money, getting even for something that might have happened thirty years ago that everyone's forgotten about by now.

Oluchi earned a whole bunch of points by shrugging and tilting his head, rather than immediately speaking.

"I'm going to go with a hard maybe, slightly in the positive, Lazarus," Oluchi said. "Both have generally done right by me, plus you and the ladies represent the possibility of trade and wealth that nobody can even calculate right now. If Ardna gets that, he steals a march on them. Upsets things here on Yisan, maybe."

"I can live with self-interest, Oluchi," Lazarus said, nodding to the man and rising. "That's an honest enough thing. Now, let's go talk to your friend."

Lazarus moved to the hatch and keyed it open, one hand close to his pistol but not quite resting on the pommel.

Xiuying Bălan was short. Five and a half feet tall in scuffed combat boots. Just about the exact minimum height for a Rio Alliance sailor. At the same time, Lazarus thought the man might outweigh him.

Small gut but not even a beer belly. Shoulders about as wide as a ship's corridor. Arms as big as Lazarus's thighs and thighs that looked like tree trunks.

Ethnic Chinese Diaspora from his face, scowling in general but not at Lazarus.

Oluchi stepped up.

"Thank you, Xiuying," he said casually.

"Gimme a chance to get back at Khan?" the small man rumbled with a smile Lazarus recognized. His eyes shifted to Lazarus. "Permission to come aboard, sir?"

"Granted," Lazarus said automatically and stepped back out of the lock.

Xiuying looked around with a perceptive, critical eye as he exited the lock and stepped into the main cargo bay.

"Been a while," he said, nodding at Lazarus.

Lazarus nodded back. Former Rio Alliance Navy, that man was. Recognized the style of the ship and knew who he was dealing with.

Xiuying knelt and unzipped the bag, pulling out a holster and a pistol wrapped in a belt.

"Didn't figure I should wear this walking around," he looked up at the two of them and smiled. "Someone might ask where the party was."

He stood and started to buckle it on.

"Need something heavier?" Lazarus asked, tapping the stock of his rifle.

"Got one amazingly similar, sir," Xiuying nodded, reaching down and pulling out a compact version.

No, his was disassembled for travel. Lazarus watched the man put three parts together and suddenly the Rio Alliance ex-marine was carrying a standard Battlerifle, a squad-level assault blaster like only the Rio Alliance Navy used. And then only for elite troopers trained for boarding actions.

"Armor?" Lazarus asked, tapping his vest.

"Covered," the man tapped his own, under the sweatshirt he wore. It made the same sound.

Xiuying turned to Oluchi.

"Got their coordinates, yet?" he asked in a cold, brutal tone.

"Waiting a few calls back," Oluchi said. "Some major players have decided to get involved."

"How major?" the man asked, his head coming up and turning a little.

"That major," Oluchi nodded.

"Gotcha," Xiuying said.

They settled back on the bridge and Lazarus's comm chirped again.

He had saved the number. Eduardo Martìnez.

"Sir?" Lazarus asked as he keyed it live.

"There will be a young woman along shortly, Lazarus," the man said. "She works for me."

And the line went dead.

Oluchi's beeped a moment later.

"Yes, sir?" Oluchi sat taller as Lazarus watched. "Yes, sir. Thank you, sir."

He lowered the comm with a look of utter and profound shock on his face.

"That was Eduardo Martìnez," Oluchi said.

"So was mine," Lazarus replied, a little confused as to why the man felt the need to call the other man immediately.

"I have the location, and Martìnez is sending us some help," Oluchi said. "Why not just tell you?"

"He wants to make sure you're involved," Lazarus guessed. "Either you've impressed him, or he's expecting you to be his point man with me after this and wants to make sure you owe him. Probably both."

"I think your ride just arrived," Xiuying spoke up suddenly, pointing out the front window at a small panel truck that had just come to land outside the immediate blast area if he were to suddenly lift off.

Lazarus watched a petite woman with dark brown skin and short, curly hair step out of the van and start to walk towards them. If you'd met her on the street, she'd catch the eyes with the grace of her walk, long muscular legs on a short torso, everything covered over with loose pants and a formless, gray jacket.

Nothing about her face stood out, being not the utter

perfection of beauty or the ragged asymmetry of ugly. Forgettable, other than those legs.

But yeah, she looked like trouble.

TWENTY-SIX

AILEEN

AILEEN MADE sure that Eha had friendly contact as they made their way down the wharf to the big boat. She'd spent enough time around Addison to know how much the average Churquen disliked open bodies of water. Even her sleeping pool back on *Shiva Zephyr Glaive* got Addison's scales in a tizzy if he came into her cabin for something.

This was a whole freaking ocean, and all these dumb goons wanted them to go aboard somebody's toy ship.

Still, Eha moved without complaint. Aileen wasn't sure what they would do if either of them refused, but Lazarus had been sent on, when they might have simply killed him, so hopefully, somebody just wanted to talk and didn't really have any solid grasp on manners.

The name of the boat, painted across the square stern as they got close to the ramp, was *Cardinal,* but she knew that with Humans it might be either the color or a bird native to their homeworld, so she wasn't sure if there were deeper meanings she was missing.

Lots of idiot birds around, yarping loudly and swooping around as they walked. White bodies with gray on the leading edge of the wings and central tail feathers. Annoying shits, but the men around them didn't seem to like the birds any more than she did.

Up the ramp. Aileen could always swim away. Humans needed complicated gear to stay underwater for any length of time, or to move quickly. But Eha would be trapped here alone.

Aileen felt the woman freeze now, just as her coil hit the bottom of the ramp. Her weight stopped Aileen as well.

"What's the problem, ladies?" the angry short man rumbled from the top of the ramp when he turned around.

"Gimme a second!" Aileen snapped at him and then turned to Eha.

The Churquen was freaking out right now. Even worse than Addison would have. Must really hate water.

"Eha, I'm with you," Aileen said calmly. "I'll stay with you. You can do this."

Aileen wasn't sure she'd ever seen a Churquen with eye slits that far open. The breath was a harsh rasp. The muscles in her tail were quivering.

"Eha?" Aileen asked as the men behind them started to stir.

"Okay," she said quietly, shivering once the whole length of her body and then starting to flow up the ramp.

"Problem?" the little man asked when they got to the top.

"Her kind don't swim," Aileen said simply.

"Oh," he replied, his voice changing down just a shade. "Not a lot of choice about that, then. Boss wanted you lot aboard his boat where he could have some privacy. Mind your step."

She followed him across the broad fantail and forward to where a space was overhung from the way the upper deck stuck out like a balcony.

Outside, everything was rugged and durable, so Aileen assumed that this planet must get some ugly storms. Once she was inside, everything turned to luxury. Polished wood inlays on the walls. Rough, hardwood floor over the deck plates. Rugs tacked down. Gold and silver filigree everywhere to offset the faint mustard color of the wall paint that made her suddenly hungry for a sandwich.

This was a space to entertain guests as they exited and went forward, turned, and descended to a lower deck dedicated to crew spaces. Raw walls in off-white. Floors that had been chewed up by boots and polished by traffic.

"In here," the man commanded, gesturing them into what Aileen discovered was a crew cabin.

Top and bottom bunks. A small desk with a Human chair. Space under the bottom bunk where a trunk could be stashed.

Nothing luxurious, just where crew slept.

The door closed and Aileen heard the lock set.

She turned to Eha and studied the woman's eyes and scales.

"You made it this far," she reminded Eha.

"Water," Eha whispered.

"You saw how many escape pods and emergency suits Lazarus had on *Ajax*, Eha," Aileen reminded her. "There were swimming rings to throw and inflatable boats on the rear deck, plus a spot below that looked like a shuttle bay down at the water level, so probably a pleasure boat with an engine that's too big. If I can find a way to blow this stupid ship up, we'll be able to get you to shore safely."

"Think it will come to that?" Eha asked, just a little life coming slowly into her voice.

"I'm sure the boys are up to something, but I'm not relying on it," Aileen replied quietly. "Whoever owns this tub could have just called and invited us to lunch."

"And now?"

"And now we wait," Aileen reassured her. "Somebody wants to talk."

She doubted they would have anything Aileen wanted to hear. She just needed time. She knew Lazarus far better than anybody else on the crew did. Far more than Eha Dunham had been able to pick up in a month.

He might look friendly and mostly harmless, but she'd seen the anger in his eyes when they got hustled back into the car and sent on their way.

These fucking morons had no idea what was coming to rescue her.

TWENTY-SEVEN
OLUCHI

OLUCHI WATCHED with the others as the small brown woman walked up. He'd always prided himself on being a casually hip kind of guy who could be dropped into any situation and make it work.

A social chameleon.

This woman looked like someone who could disappear into the background and be completely invisible, even in a Chinese Diaspora nudist colony. Everything about her screamed silence.

Or whatever the opposite of scream was. Deathly silence.

She reminded him of a ghost.

"Pryce," she said with a nod to him as she stepped close and looked up at Lazarus. "Eduardo sent me."

She had a voice that might have come from a computer system. Again, one of those designed to sound helpful without being so sexy that they distracted you.

Oluchi understood what the woman did for Eduardo now, and it didn't involve keeping his bed warm.

"Lazarus," the man replied firmly, obviously inspecting her, but not as a man might a woman, not like Oluchi had.

Like a navy captain making sure a new sailor was up to snuff. Lazarus had that look about him, regardless of the vague deflections he had offered earlier when asked.

"Xiuying," the other man rumbled with an extremely polite smile, like he had seen this woman, or another of her species come into his bar and immediately called a few off-duty bouncers to come on duty, just in case.

"Grace Savidge," she replied with a nod.

"Weapons?" Lazarus asked simply.

"What gear I need is in the van," she said coolly.

Oluchi took that to mean that she was a weapon herself, and had a few housebreaking tools and maybe a radio over there.

Ninja, maybe. Something equivalent.

Scary.

Her smile in his direction suggested that she was also reading his mind. Or he had forgotten to put his poker face on.

He fixed that oversight and nodded to her.

"Eduardo told me that you'd know where to go," Grace looked at all of them in sequence, like she was measuring them, before settling on Lazarus.

Good guess, but wrong here.

"Ardna apparently took them down to the harbor and put them aboard *Cardinal*, his yacht," Oluchi said, "Then sailed out past the breakwater but didn't go anywhere."

"Six hours of darkness until false dawn," Grace observed neutrally. "Fortunate that it is winter and the days are longer. Do we assume a friendly misunderstanding on their part when we arrive?"

"The two women that were kidnapped at gunpoint are two different alien species nobody on this planet has ever met before," Lazarus replied in a voice starting to betray the rage Oluchi had seen earlier. "One of them is humanoid from the waist up and giant snake below that. The other is a four and a half foot tall otter. Ardna reacted very negatively towards the first, Eha Dunham, and rumors suggest a fear of snakes in general."

"Okay," Grace nodded more as a placeholder than anything.

Oluchi found himself joining the other two staring at the newcomer expectantly.

"I don't like guns being pointed at me," Lazarus said. "Where I come from kidnapping someone is generally a capital offense. I doubt the laws are so strict here, but if anything happens to those two women, my suggestion would be for the three of you to get off-planet as quickly as possible, because the assistance I would go get in that case includes seven other species and enough firepower to end Yisan as an inhabited planet. Eha's mate is likely to use it. I'd be happy to help him. I will ask them once. Only once. Then I will kill every single one of them that are involved. That clean enough for your rules of engagement?"

"Not even asking Khan once," Xiuying rumbled. "The rest'll maybe get a chance ta drop guns afores I splatter 'em."

"Good enough," Grace said with a nod Oluchi could only qualify as *serene*.

He wondered what he had gotten himself into, but that was a shallow question. He'd walked in from the beginning understanding that this situation might be the biggest thing to happen in his lifetime, and a chance to get rich enough that he never had to hustle again.

Unless he wanted to.

"There are three ways onto, or off of, a boat in the middle of the ocean," Oluchi found himself saying. "Fly out and land. Sail out on a boat. Both of those make noise and are likely to get someone's attention. The other involves a bit of a swim. Probably the quietest way."

"I have gear for three arranged," Grace said, turning to eye Xiuying. "I will make a call as we drive and get you fitted out. Gentlemen, shall we?"

Oluchi nodded and tried to pretend that he was just as dangerous as these three killers he found himself getting into a van with.

But really, he figured he was about as dangerous as a flyswatter trying to stop a charging water buffalo. Fortunately, he was on the water buffalo's side.

TWENTY-EIGHT

LAZARUS

THE FLIGHT to oceanside went quickly as Lazarus sat in the front seat and watched. Grace handled the controls like any of the best boatswains he had ever flown with, and kept them out over the hills, rather than blasting noisily down the highway, where someone might look up and wonder. Or maybe be watching and make a call.

Lazarus had known that bringing Eha and Aileen here was a risk, but he'd deemed it a political risk, not a personal one.

However, that man that had stopped their car, Khan was apparently his name, had said he'd kill them if they gave him any grief, so Lazarus didn't feel like he was overreacting to the situation.

You could have called and invited us to a private lunch, my friend. Might have come. Might not have. But now, you've got an enemy with an impossibly long memory. Three if you do something stupid, because Eduardo won't get his trade and Addison probably won't stop until he smashes your entire corporation into the mud and then hunts down every ship you own and shatters it.

The Rio Alliance Navy plays by the rules, but I'm not Pancho Oliveira anymore. My name is Lazarus of Bethany, and I'm a wanted man in Innruld space.

Grace was watching him out of the corner of her eye as she flew. He glanced over and stared until she talked.

"Aliens?" she asked finally.

"Churquen and Yithadreph," Lazarus replied. "Back at the ship are Necherle, Kr'mari, Qooph, Tarni, Vaadwig, and Ilount. And a warship. A big, dangerous one."

She nodded.

Lazarus noted that the woman didn't have a single wasted motion. Everything was precise and specific. Chatter was at a minimum as well. Just enough to cover the details or ask questions. Nothing more.

The two men in the back of the van were having a low conversation, but there was no laughter, so probably planning. Oluchi Pryce had never been aboard the *Cardinal*, but there were only so many ways to build something that size. From the descriptions the woman had brought, *Cardinal* wasn't much larger than the sort of cutters he had commanded when he was a punk kid fifteen years ago.

"What does it mean when aliens come to Yisan?" Grace asked.

Lazarus was surprised. She moved and spoke like an assassin most of the time, but he hadn't seen anything suggesting the depths of education and knowledge necessary to make that intellectual leap, so she had many more layers than he had expected.

"Trade, possibly," Lazarus said. "I'm heading to Brasilia, but they wanted the chance to see Humanity in the raw, before everything became a highly-scripted event with protocol and diplomatic standards. Eduardo's on my good list, as is Fernanda Flores. Ardna is not."

"Who are you really, Lazarus?" she turned her head fully

to stare at him and dropped her voice to the point that the others wouldn't hear, but he figured the autopilot was up to the task of flying, if it came to that.

"Rio Alliance Navy," he said simply. "I was testing an experimental warship when I had to flee for my life. A group of random aliens rescued me, got me back on my feet, and then protected me from folks like Strav Ardna back where they come from. They're in the process of taking me home to get some help smashing their own fools, and I'll assist when we get there."

"And fools who get in your way here?" Grace asked.

"Eduardo and Fernanda I'll protect from Eha's mate as much as I can," Lazarus offered. "I was trying to show my friends the good sides of Humanity. That appears to have been a mistake on my part."

"Maybe not," she glanced back to include Oluchi and Xiuying in her observation.

"Maybe not," he relented. "I appear to have made some friends here, as well."

She had a pretty smile. He saw it now for a brief flash before she returned to a default neutrality.

"Strav Ardna isn't usually this stupid," she volunteered. "But that's not the same as saying he's never done stupid things. Is he trying to torture information out of the women?"

"Is that within his realm?" Lazarus asked with a chill he couldn't shake off. Then the rage ignited again. "Does he do that when he doesn't get his way?"

"Occasionally," Grace nodded. "Eduardo doesn't keep me on staff just for my tea making ability and musical talents."

She glanced over now, and must have read the confusion there.

"Geisha didn't always just mean highly-paid prostitute, or performer in a historical reenactment," she said, her face as deadly serious as her voice was quiet. "Once upon a time, it was one of the best covers a woman could have, when she worked in certain other fields."

"Assassin," Lazarus breathed back at her.

She nodded.

"Perhaps I'll also be lucky enough to hear you sing sometime," Lazarus offered obliquely, suggesting that there would likely be killing soon.

Unplumbed depths, like a black pearl hidden in a pile of coal.

She studied him closer now, eyes narrow and judgmental.

Weighing his soul?

"Perhaps," she offered back.

Again, the ghost of a smile, gone before it registered anywhere except his memory.

Then she turned her attention back to flying and Lazarus lapsed into his brooding.

Maybe he had found friends on Yisan after all.

He absolutely had an enemy.

Briefly.

AILEEN WAS surprised when they came for her alone, but she didn't get much chance to ask questions. The short Human with the growly voice threw open the door, gestured in her direction with a gun, and smiled.

"Only you, princess," he said gruffly.

Eha had stirred on the bottom bunk, but subsided and the Humans locked the door again, with Aileen in the corridor surrounded by men. Tall men.

It was really getting to be annoying, being surrounded by storks all the damned time.

They marched her forward and up a deck, towards the bow. This deck ended in a double door that Growlyboy knocked on and then opened.

They entered and Aileen found herself in a room as wide as the hull, with dark windows on both sides and wood furniture representing a serious amount of cash to have custom made.

Carpets almost as thick and soft as her pelt underfoot. More polished wood and inlay, with lots of gold and silver work. Sofas on one side, chairs and a desk on the other.

And one old Human seated behind the desk. The one from the party. The rude shit who'd stomped out early in the evening without a word to anyone.

That guy.

Aileen didn't particularly like that guy.

He gestured for her to sit in the chair in front of him on her right. The stupid, Human chair made for someone who was all legs and no tail.

Aileen kept her grumble to herself and climbed up. The guy had half a dozen goons with him, and not all of them had guns out, so she figured someone would tackle her before she could rip the guy's throat out with her teeth.

Always an option when a woman decides to tell you no, buddy.

"We weren't properly introduced earlier," he said in a hard voice trying to sound polite as Aileen finished *climbing up the stupid, fucking chair meant for someone with legs as long as Lazarus who didn't ALSO have a tail.* "Strav Ardna."

"Aileen Enjehn," she replied, fidgeting until she found a spot that didn't hurt her butt.

"What are you…people?" he demanded.

Aileen had caught the stutter. That moment when someone wanted to use a less friendly term.

She presumed this son of a diseased galumph was Westphalian originally, or had at least picked up all the beliefs in Human supremacy. It had all been theoretical before, listening to Lazarus explain things, but shit just got visceral tonight.

"Traders," Aileen evaded the question bluntly. "Lazarus was adrift in space when we pulled him into our airlock. Got him fixed up and introduced to some of the folks back where we come from, then brought him back to Human space so he could get home."

And that was even true, as long as you skipped over the

part where a nervous Ilount doofus had blown up Lazarus's ship in the first place and nearly killed the Human aboard.

Not that she had ever stopped teasing Wybert about it. Kept him humble.

Oh, and she also skipped a warship with a really, freaking dangerous boomstick on the front.

"Back home?" Ardna asked with a slight gasp. "How many worlds do you represent?"

Ah, the trade question.

Are you furry, scaly weirdoes big enough to threaten us, or small enough we can roll over you and suddenly gain a whole new nest of slaves and servants?

Aileen really didn't like his tone of voice. It helped to imagine the Human as a short, balding Innruld who had worked himself into a lather on something. Then they might be cousins.

Asshole cousins, but you know…

"About a thousand, last I checked," Aileen lied coldly at the bastard. "North of forty different species, not counting regional variants in biology."

Might has well whomp you upside the head now, eh?

Worked. The Human went pale. Must *really* not like aliens or something.

"And you're here for trade?" he demanded, voice starting to gain some of the strength she expected from a merchant.

Never let attitude problems get in the way of making money.

"I am, but I'm not in charge," she smiled warmer now, imagining Eha or Addison wrapping this fool up in their coils and squeezing him slowly. Oh so slowly. "I'm just the ship's Quartermaster, brought along to handle cargo loading and such."

She let her whiskers and ears telegraph bright-eyed innocence at the man, just to rub it in a little more.

"And the other two?" he barked. "The Human and that *thing*?"

Ah. Snake terrors. Got it.

Lazarus had warned them. Apparently, they'd found one.

"Lazarus wanted to stop here to show off," Aileen said simply. "Then the ship's headed to Brasilia to talk to the government there."

"What kind of ship?" his voice fell to a hollow whisper.

Brass tacks and shipping schedules time, buddy?

"Incredibly well-armed warship, at least as I understand your standards," she grinned, waggling her whiskers now at the joke in her head. "Lazarus is the only Human. Rest of the crew are all aliens like me. Well, not just like me. You got Qooph, Vaadwig, Necherle, Kr'mari, Yithadreph like me, and the commander's a Churquen like Eha."

All of that is technically true, your honor. Sins of omission don't count if bald guy over there's not smart enough to ask the right questions. Always got told to never volunteer things to cops and bureaucrats by my momma.

"More of those things?" he almost squealed as he hissed in a breath.

"Yeah," Aileen agreed innocently. Close enough to innocently, anyway. "Churquen are actually the single largest species, by numbers, I think."

Gosh, it was fun watching him squirm.

"And the other one is in charge here?" he snarled, whiplashing through his emotions almost too fast for a girl to follow.

"Yup. She's the Ambassador to the Humans."

Aileen sat back against the seat, in spite of how much it hurt her stubby tail to do that. Looked better, conveying total cool to a worked up Human.

Lazarus had warned her.

She'd been nervous that the dork had some sort of

strange fetish, but it wasn't snakes. And he wasn't totally Human supremacist, or he probably would have kidnapped Lazarus and shot them.

Doesn't make you any less of an asshole, buddy.

Still, ears neutral. Whiskers relaxed. Waiting politely for your high-and-mightiness to get over himself and ask a better series of questions. Smarter ones.

Aileen smiled to herself, thinking about the six months she'd spent wondering what her first encounter with Humans without Lazarus around would be like.

Now, she knew.

Good thing you took my pistol, buddy, and have enough guys around that I can't come across that desk and break your neck before they get to me.

Different adventure then.

"Ambassador?" he whispered in a tone she could only ascribe to pure horror. "No."

Aileen fought to keep her whiskers from betraying her.

She watched the change come over the Human. Gone was the panic. Rage had taken its place. She and Eha were suddenly standing under a stack of boxes that were about to tip over on top of them, them just watching it lean.

Aileen suspected that she might be collateral damage, but this bastard was going to kill Eha, just as soon as he worked up the courage.

The strange part was balancing the greed in his soul against the hatred. Aileen had made it clear that she couldn't help navigate them somewhere, since she really didn't have a clue about the coordinates, only the direction and distance. Eha was the key to Innruld space, although she wasn't about to mention that to this jerk.

He was the type Lazarus had feared would make common cause with the Innruld. Furless bipeds against everyone else, and all that. Human technology over there in

Innruld hands and the Species Underground would never break free.

Aileen kept her mouth shut.

Up until now, she'd been pushing, just a little bit, mostly to keep him off balance. He didn't have murder in his eyes, but it wasn't that far removed now. Anything she said might tip him over into doing something reckless and irretrievable.

She waited.

He stood now and she couldn't help tensing, but he moved to a side window and stared out it for a long minute, like he was alone in here.

She didn't even breathe too loudly, on the off-chance he forgot she was here, or maybe had a heart attack and keeled over dead while she watched.

Either would be an improvement on the situation.

Finally, he turned back. Stared at her with hatred in his eyes so overwhelming that any veneer of civility vanished for a second.

"Return her to the cabin," he snarled at the men around him.

Aileen slipped off the chair and landed on her feet as Growlyboy appeared from behind her and thumbed her towards the door.

She moved without pause, glancing back over her shoulder only at the hatch, but old bald guy had returned to staring out the window.

Working up the courage.

They'd have to go down fighting, when the Humans came for Eha.

Bastards.

THIRTY

LAZARUS

THERE WAS a man that met them when they landed near the docks, but Lazarus never heard a name and Grace didn't introduce him. Xiuying got fitted out for a drysuit quickly and everyone got scuba gear and helmets.

Lazarus was EVA qualified, so he wasn't completely lost, nor was Xiuying, but Oluchi needed help with everything. Not much, though.

Lazarus got the impression he'd done friendly dives with pretty ladies like Fernanda at some point. Just never with blasters, or at night.

To kill people.

Just like the Rio Alliance Navy days.

Grace checked his equipment after doing Oluchi, while the stranger got Xiuying fixed up. She was startled as she ran hands over everything.

Like surprised a Rio Alliance Navy officer wasn't incompetent.

He smiled down at her and she nodded wryly back.

"They moved?" Grace asked the stranger that had joined them.

"Nope," he answered with a rough drawl. "Parked about three miles out with the engines off and all the lights on."

Grace turned back to him and Lazarus saw something in her eyes he couldn't identify.

"We'll approach from the seaside," she said. "Running dark where we don't get backlit by anything, and then drop into the ocean a mile out with a sled and approach underwater. Any of you ever done something like this before?"

"Never," Oluchi said, bravely willing to just leap out of a van into the ocean in the middle of the night.

"Not officially," Xiuying spoke up in an ambiguous tone that still caught her head around.

Grace turned to him and Lazarus smiled.

"It wasn't water," Lazarus offered.

She squinted up at him and then nodded.

"Everyone into the van and let's do this thing," she said simply.

Lazarus followed her, trying not to be distracted by watching the woman move.

Inside the van was a sled that reminded him of an EVA scooter. Same basic principle, except that this one used water jets instead of compressed propellant.

Grace's friend climbed up front and they lifted off smoothly, heading south into the night.

After a time where everyone sat in silence with their own thoughts, Grace leaned forward to talk to the driver.

"Take us out here and shut down all the lights, including interior," she ordered.

Lazarus checked both his weapons and then stuffed them into a sealed bag and slung it across his back. The others did the same.

"When we hit water, I will attach all of you to the sled by cords around your hand and wrist," Grace continued. "I'll drive the sled and your job is to not fall off and make us come back for you. Since none of you have been aboard *Cardinal* before, I'll take the lead when we get there. I note that nobody but me has a stunner?"

"I'm planning to play rough," Lazarus explained simply. "Nobody has taught this man better manners before now. Time for him to learn."

"Whatever," Xiuying chimed in. "Killing Khan if I get a chance."

"Oluchi?" Grace asked, her own dark skin betraying no emotions.

"Eduardo pointedly put me here," the gambler replied. "Guess that means I might be killing folks tonight. Pretty sure they've got it coming. Some of them, anyway."

"I see," Grace looked at all of them in turn before she returned to Lazarus. "We'll play it your way."

He could see unasked questions in her eyes. Like why they were going straight to violence, rather than negotiating, but he could also tell that Eduardo had told her to listen to the stranger and follow his orders.

Lazarus was just trying to prevent an even-greater incident from occurring. Addison would already have to be talked out of an orbital bombardment event later, even if Ardna let Eha and Aileen go right now with an abject apology.

Lazarus was just sad that he'd never run into someone that made him feel the same way as Eha obviously did about Addison. And vice versa.

Thing went dark as they turned and headed to sea. Quickly enough, the van came to a hover.

"Close enough," the driver said. "Wind starting to come up from seaward and forecast suggests a pretty nasty storm just before dawn."

"You get some coffee after this," Grace said. "I'll signal where we need a pickup, but you might need to come fast."

"Whelan's Cove?" he replied.

"Good enough," Grace said.

She opened the side door and shoved the sled out.

Lazarus watched it fall about ten feet and hit the waves with a huge splash. Grace was out a moment later, knifing into the water like her name.

Lazarus turned to Oluchi and nodded him out, probably the least trained for water emergencies of all of them, if he had to guess. Xiuying laughed and went next, cannonballing into the water like Lazarus just knew he would.

Then it was his turn. He checked his helmet and air. Confirmed the system temperature, seals, and his weapons. Lazarus slipped out and hung in the air before dropping so softly his helmet stayed dry.

Then he descended into the darkness like a swimming predator.

THIRTY-ONE
OLUCHI

THIS WAS nothing like diving a reef with Fernanda, or any of the other pretty girls he'd known. However, Oluchi was willing to admit, in the privacy of his own head, that people weren't necessarily wrong to imply he was a gigolo and a dilettante. Handsome, charming, and smart had gotten him so many more interesting places than hard work and clean living ever suggested.

Tonight, though, he might end up an actual killer, and not just a lady-killer.

The water was dark and calm when Grace got them all below the surface. It was a whole other world from fun dives in shallow waters with pretty women.

They descended a few yards into the hollow, dark silence, broken only by his breathing inside the helmet and the pounding of his heart wanting to break bodily out of his chest.

Nobody had fins, so Grace pulled loops from inside the sled and wrapped the cord loosely around his wrist, then physically put both his hands on a rail designed to haul people like him. Xiuying and Lazarus got themselves taken care of, and Grace powered the sled up, flying them through the night looking at a screen he could just make out.

It only showed one target, slowly approaching as they knifed through the water, which was good. Yisan had a few predatory aquatic species, both mammalian and piscine in nature, that got freaking huge. Large enough to swallow the whole party in a single gulp, although Oluchi suspected that the other three would just kill the creature from the inside and cut their bloody way out before continuing on their way without so much as a *by your leave*.

He wasn't sure if he should be frightened by the prospect of being in the company of such merciless people, or excited. Yesterday seemed like years ago and tomorrow felt like an eternity away. But he was here, now, and certainly Oluchi Pryce had reached an age where he was going to have to make changes soon.

The ladies would begin to notice the younger ones one of these days. Rugged and handsome would start looking less appealing as he crossed forty and began to show his years. His options would start getting narrower and less interesting.

He'd eventually get desperate enough…

No, better to open a new door here. Eduardo had specifically hung up on Lazarus to call Oluchi Pryce and give him the coordinates, so that the man had someone he knew in a position to influence outcomes.

Hopefully, Oluchi would be able to parley that into a permanent gig, presumably with Lazarus and the others, being a personal representative to the Human tycoons of Yisan.

Fixer.

Kind of the opposite of what he'd been doing all his life, being the thing bored and lonely housewives with money found, but maybe he just needed to stop being a gigolo and move up a little. After all, a fixer was just a pimp with a wider clientele. Not that much would change.

He kept his snort of derision personal, lest Grace or one of the others think he was suffering some sort of troubles. Physical troubles, anyway, as opposed to moral ones.

Quickly enough, lights began to appear in the distance. Grace turned the sled upwards and they broached the surface to find a storm starting to patter them with rain drops.

Grace popped her facemask open, so he did as well. The other two joined them.

"If we get much closer underneath, their sonar will probably notice us," she said simply. "Not sure how keyed up or paranoid they might be, but approaching on the surface now is a better bet."

"Leave the sled?" Lazarus asked.

"We can always come back for it, or program it to return to shore," she shrugged.

"Good enough," Lazarus growled. "Let's board and have a conversation with those folks about salon manners."

Oluchi felt a shiver run down his spine at the tone. Lazarus had been calm and a touch distant earlier, as one would expect with a recently-met stranger showing only-barely-ulterior motives.

The ride in the underwater darkness had apparently turned him into a sea monster from a horror vid.

He watched the others close up their facemasks again and dive, so Oluchi joined them after taking a moment to study *Cardinal,* all of about thirty yards away now and lit up like daylight. At least there was nobody standing on the fantail at the moment.

What sensors might record a pod of sharks approaching, or a tribe of sea monsters boarding, remained yet to be seen.

Somehow, Oluchi didn't think Lazarus or the others cared that much.

THIRTY-TWO

LAZARUS

IT HADN'T BEEN WATER, but Lazarus had done something like this before. After all, he hadn't always been a respected *Capitão De Mar E Guerra*. Once upon a time, a much younger *Pancho* Oliveira had worked for the Special Branches Section in the Field Division, rather than over in Research & Development.

Doing the sorts of things that he wouldn't be cleared to discuss with people until thirty years after he was dead. That was always the inside joke with the teams. *Been there, done that* had a whole other connotation that could cover a multitude of sins and memories without ever admitting anything.

Underwater, Grace moved like an eel. Lazarus felt awkward by comparison, until he looked at the other two. She was just simply in another category beyond him.

That would make the rest of this even easier.

Cardinal was immense. Over a hundred yards long, and built more bulky than sleek. A floating casino, perhaps, rather than a saber cutting through the water. He could hear the purring hum of station-keeping water jets holding the ship against tide and swell, but they would have to cut the engines in soon, if the storm kept rising.

That or drop an anchor. He would have preferred a rope to climb right now. Better than coming up the stern ladder. Less likely to be noticed by a Human or a systems alarm.

Hopefully, they were already moving so fast tonight that the kidnappers weren't expecting trouble.

What were the chances that a stranger to this planet could recruit this level of firepower and technology on the fly? Presumably low, if you were expecting the man to be a shipwrecked sailor without the folks rescuing him.

Lazarus stole a look at Oluchi, swimming nearby. A change had come over the man, just in the half day Lazarus had known him. The gambler had been all *bon vivant* at dinner and the party. Seriousness had crept up on him. Hopefully, it would hold and he wouldn't fold in the clutch.

Grace signaled for them to remain below, illuminated now by the surface lights. He watched her surface just enough of her face to retract the mask and watch, before closing back up and dropping down.

She signaled the other two to remain below and for him to surface, so Lazarus went up and looked.

They were just off the starboard rear of the ship. Not far from the fantail and the ladder, currently folded up but easily reachable.

Climbable.

Nobody was visible on the deck above, or the porch deck above that. Rain was falling harder now, the mist thickening to something rough enough that most people would want to remain indoors.

Hopefully, that would work to his advantage.

Grace surfaced and retracted her mask, so he did.

"When we touch the ladder, a clock starts," she said in a

low, hard voice, almost close enough in the surf that they could be dancing.

Or other things.

"Am I leading or you?" Lazarus asked simply.

"I'll lead," she said. "I have a stunner as well as the heavier stuff, so I can fire on movement rather than waiting to identify a target. Are you really prepared to kill people?"

"Are you?" he rasped back. "Those are my friends. Someone kidnapped them at gunpoint. After we get them back, the question will be whether or not I blow the boat up while leaving, with everyone aboard. By living on this planet, you people have chosen to be pirates. Outlaws, literally outside the law itself. You don't get to complain if someone else comes along and uses that against you. If you want Rio Alliance law, you become Rio Alliance citizens first."

She studied his face for a long second before she spoke.

"Not many people get that, Lazarus," she observed. "Everyone around here acts civilized, but it's mostly a front for some ugly rough and tumble. Like, why Eduardo keeps me on staff."

"Eduardo keeps you around because he's a smart man and you might be the most dangerous Human I've ever met, Grace," Lazarus turned to look at her from almost close enough to kiss.

She blinked in surprise, whites of her eyes standing out against the darkness of her skin.

Didn't deny it, though. Shrugged.

"Yeah," she finally agreed. "I'll get the others. You get ready to climb with me."

Lazarus nodded, touching his bag once like a lucky charm. If he didn't do this now, Addison might do something infinitely worse.

And Director Wolcott had the means at his fingertips, if he wanted. And the crew that would follow.

Three heads surfaced around him. The worsening rain was cutting visibility down to maybe twenty yards. Waves were starting to swell harder. *Cardinal* would probably fire up her engines shortly.

It was now or never.

THIRTY-THREE

OLUCHI

OLUCHI WASN'T sure he was ready to be a sea monster, but that seemed to be the only option left at this point.

Well, he could always duck back underwater, swim to shore, and go back to a declining lifestyle of debauchery, probably already sliding off the peaks of wealth and power he'd once had access to. The story would get out, marking him as a coward only good for combat in the bedroom.

Oluchi Pryce didn't want to think about becoming that person, so he waited at the bottom of the ladder as the other three climbed onto the rear deck and spread out.

He joined, taking a moment to open his sealed bag and pull out a heavier pistol than a dandy like him usually carried. Lighter weapons didn't kill unless you got lucky, and that was useful on a planet where duels were still legal.

Someone might come along and finally take exception, finding that Oluchi had bedded his wife or mistress. Actually, they would take exception when he showed the woman how much better she could have demanded earlier. Some men just didn't understand how to please a woman. It was more than just pleasuring her, but it started there.

Actually listening when she spoke. Remembering little details.

Having a thought for something beyond themselves.

The others chucked their water-tight bags over the side, having extracted a frightening arsenal of death, so Oluchi took a deep breath and did the same. Helmets remained on, but masks got retracted.

Sea monsters, dripping salty water onto the deck in gray bodysuits.

"This way," the tiny black woman said as she led the group to the starboard side of the vessel and up a quick flight of steps. Oluchi was last, for now, when they got up to the flying bridge, but it was empty.

The rains were starting to get nasty. He couldn't remember if he'd seen the weather forecast, but this felt bigger than just a fall rain coming on. Yisan didn't get hurricanes, like some planets did, but all that water out there let some monsters get a long, running start.

"When we open this hatch, a light probably goes on, if it already hasn't from us boarding," Grace said simply. "If it moves, I'm shooting it. If it shoots back, you engage. Xiuying, take the rear position, because at some point they'll successfully flank up and we'll be fighting both directions. Questions?"

Oluchi grunted with the two men and watched the lithe woman move, trying to emulate the grace she embodied with her name. She had to be a dancer, on top of everything else.

The hatch she opened was solid, rather than transparent. That was good, because she fired two quick shots and then drew the rest of them in.

Oluchi closed the door to find two men out cold on the deck, and the bridge of *Cardinal* in their hands. He followed Lazarus over to the left, where a man had spilled out of a chair, but Oluchi's eyes were on the console he had left operational.

Internal security monitors.

Lazarus started to touch something, but Oluchi caught his hand.

"Allow me," he said, sliding his bottom onto the warm seat and toggling a few things.

Four monitors showed cabins and hallways as he flipped around. Oluchi recognized one of the cabins as a place he had slept, and wondered just how much blackmail Ardna had accumulated, if he was able to tape what were supposedly private quarters.

He suppressed a growl and kept checking.

There. Aileen. Flat on a bed. Unmoving.

Behind him, Lazarus hissed.

Oluchi caught the hand that stabbed at a button and shifted the monitors with his other hand. Lazarus wrestled with him for a moment.

"She's asleep, Lazarus," he said as the vital monitors came up.

Heartrate. Body temperature.

Oluchi had no idea what might be normal for the furry woman, but she wasn't dead. Right now, that might be the only thing keeping Lazarus from cutting the throats of the two men Grace and Xiuying were tucking into a corner.

"Where?" Lazarus growled in a voice only vaguely Human.

Oluchi checked. He'd actually slept in the next cabin over on a jaunt with a cute redhead, a year ago or so. He turned to catch Grace's eye.

"B-deck," he said simply. "Cabin nine."

"Where's Eha?" Lazarus pressed. "Where's Ardna?"

Toggle. Study. Flip.

"I can't find them," Oluchi said finally.

Lazarus's face got ugly, but Oluchi forestalled him.

"But I also can't see C-1, Lazarus," Oluchi said. "That's his suite, up a deck from Aileen and all the way forward. Salon, sleeping chamber, closet, restroom."

"Good enough, for now," Grace said. "We need to get all the way down to B-deck aft."

"What's there?" Lazarus asked, but Oluchi already knew.

"The armory," she said with an angrier voice than he'd heard earlier tonight.

Made sense. Some of the men would be armed, but if they could keep the rest of the crew from getting guns, it made things much easier.

"Can you disable the console?" Lazarus pointed. "And would it matter?"

"This is the primary," Grace said. "There are a few others, but none with this level of sophistication."

"Good enough," Lazarus smiled cruelly. "Oluchi, stand clear."

He had no idea what the man was going to do, so he stood and slid to the side like a woman's husband had just opened the front door downstairs.

Lazarus fired into the console with his heavier beam, shattering it with a whoop of energy and a small shower of sparks.

"Xiuying, are you capable of ripping the steering wheel off the post so they can't go anywhere?" Lazarus turned to the dangerous dwarf.

Xiuying smiled and reached into a pocket.

"I can do you one better," he said as he pulled out a powertorque.

Oluchi watched the man kneel and back out the bolts holding the wheel on, then pocketing them while whistling under his breath.

That was certainly not something Oluchi had expected, but they all had hidden depths.

He watched Grace open the hatch forward, where he remembered the main stairwell down, and wondered what depths he might find inside himself.

Tonight, he just might have to.

JUVENILE DELINQUENCY DIDN'T DEFRAY the rage pounding in his chest, but blowing up the security console had knocked some of the edges off, and Lazarus was more confident he wouldn't overreact now.

If that was possible.

Oluchi caught him by the arm as Grace scouted the next chamber.

"Why the violence, Lazarus?" he had apparently finally worked up the courage to ask.

All night, the man had been just running on a wet, tumbling log, from the body language, but things were getting imminent.

"Eha's mate is in command of a warship capable of obliterating any security forces in orbit of this planet," Lazarus told him in a low rumble. "If something happens to her, he might start shooting at surface targets when he's done with that. There are a few people on this planet I would miss, if the Churquen decided to kill everyone. And he might. I'd like to stop that, but people who show up with guns like that don't understand that there might be bigger guns until it gets out of hand."

"This isn't out of hand?" Oluchi indicated the whole ship, something short of panic on his face, but well-concealed.

Better than Lazarus had expected.

"Leveling Tershuvi with energy weapons from orbit might not be out of hand for Addison Wolcott, Oluchi," Lazarus said.

He watched the man blink in surprise.

Never had consequences, have you?

Lazarus wasn't surprised. For a gambler, Oluchi Pryce acted a lot like a high-class call girl.

Still, he was here. He had put on the drysuit and come with them. He was holding a gun in his hand.

And he had asked.

Something came over the man now. A settling, for lack of a better term to call it.

Oluchi Pryce's shoulders came down at the same time his chin came up and his breath flowed out.

The pretty playboy with the suave words seemed to disappear like a shade being drawn.

"I'd like to prevent that," he said simply. Firmly. "Eduardo, as you noted, is counting on me to protect his interests, so perhaps we'll be able to settle for just killing Strav Ardna. Certainly the galaxy would be a better place."

Lazarus was shocked to his core, watching another man take root in that flesh, but he'd only known the gigolo for a day. Maybe Oluchi Pryce was capable of growing up, and had just never found the reason.

Damsels in distress would be as good as anything.

"Are you two done?" Grace hissed from the doorway.

Lazarus studied Oluchi for a moment and found what he wanted. He turned to Grace and nodded.

In his hands, he still cradled the blaster rifle, and that

seemed to fit his mood. Xiuying smiled with his even heavier weapon.

Violence was in the air like the charge before a storm.

Or the center of the storm outside.

Grace moved. Flowed.

Lazarus was silent behind her, and still felt like a clumsy ox as he watched her in motion. Oluchi had apparently gained experience in silence at some point as well.

Probably coming and going through boudoir windows, but Lazarus didn't even think that too loud. The man was here, and willing. Hopefully capable. Xiuying was also here, and dangerous.

They could do this.

Grace paused at the first level down and waited for him to catch up.

"C-deck," she whispered, gesturing. "Down one more."

Lazarus nodded and checked. They were in a spiral staircase, so the space was almost a closet, but that made it compact enough that someone would have to be right in the hallway, standing next to them, to see anyone.

Downside, a crew member might walk right up on them before they could do anything.

Lazarus nodded to Xiuying and indicated he should watch here. The man nodded and Lazarus circled down after Grace, Oluchi right behind him.

B-deck was nowhere as luxurious as C-deck had been, which made a crude sense. The parties occurred on C-deck and above, so that's where the guests would be. If you were important enough to stay for a weekend, you might have a cabin up there. If you were a nobody or crew, Ardna could put you below.

Grace was peeking out of the stairwell on B-deck, with Lazarus just around the coil from her. She motioned him closer and slipped partway into the hall so he could get close.

It was still a crowded fit. He was almost dancing with the woman in the tight confines. They were certainly close enough to kiss, had they wanted. Her wry smile of acknowledgment almost made him blush.

"You watch forward," she whispered. "I'll take Pryce and disable the lock on the armory, so nobody can open it quickly."

Lazarus nodded and slipped across the hallway to a slightly recessed door. Grace said something to Oluchi which caused him to slip back up the stairs, and return a moment later with Xiuying.

They were all down here now. He didn't like to think that they were trapped, because the hull of the ship itself looked to be a carbon-fiber monocast and he and the ex-marine had weapons heavy enough to blast a hole through if they needed out.

It was mostly psychological.

He watched forward. Xiuying watched up the shaft. Oluchi joined Grace and did something esoteric, hunched over the keypad to a door next to the stairwell aft.

Steps coming down from above caused Xiuying to signal intruders.

Lazarus motioned him to step to the right, and he moved a little closer to the bow, just outside the stairwell where he could watch and listen.

One man from the weight of the treads. Not in a hurry. Not trying to be quiet. Heavy boots, rather than the sort of softer shoes you wore on a ship's deck, and presumably a maritime yacht as well.

Soldier.

No, goon. Those men had been thugs with guns.

Lazarus smiled, hoping he might recognize the man when he appeared.

Pause as the man arrived on B-deck and turned.

Movement as he stepped out and turned towards Xiuying.

Lazarus hammered him at the base of the skull with the butt of his blaster rifle.

Didn't think he overdid it. The sound was softer than chucking a watermelon out a third story window to land on pavement below.

The man went down like a sack of potatoes at Xiuying's feet. The marine grinned and slung his own rifle, already up for a solid butt-stroke to the chin.

Zip ties appeared from another of the bouncer's pockets. Got used. Target got neutralized.

Silence.

Oluchi and Grace had reacted to the noise, and then gone back to what they were doing.

Lazarus kept watch all directions. The boat creaked and pitched worse than it had.

Disabling the cockpit permanently might cause troubles in another hour, but Lazarus didn't plan to be here that long.

Oluchi rose with a walk that reminded Lazarus of a cheetah with a bloody muzzle, from having run down some prey and killed it. Lazarus blinked and recalibrated his opinion of the man up a notch.

Again.

"They will need a fire ax to get in there now," Oluchi assured him as the man came close, grinning.

Lazarus grinned back.

Grace slid past them, again closer to Lazarus than she needed to be, brushing herself against his side when she could have passed without any contact. Oluchi followed her, and Lazarus came third, leaving Xiuying watching the rear still.

Pryce stopped the small woman a little forward and

touched a hatch lightly. Lazarus was close enough to hear him whisper.

"Small boat launch here in a water well," he said.

Ah. A shuttle for the big ship, capable of taking you to the dock, rather like bringing someone down from orbit, since *Ajax* could never land on a planetary surface.

That would make escape easier to plan for, if they could just steal a boat.

Just forward of that, Grace and Oluchi stopped and started working on a panel.

Cabin nine.

Aileen.

Lazarus moved past them and aimed at the bow, just daring someone to step out right now. His safety was still off.

The two thieves worked quickly while Lazarus listened.

The lock opened and Grace touched him on the arm.

"She won't know us," the dark woman said with a smile. "You go first."

Lazarus nodded and handed Grace his rifle. She looked at him, maybe a little surprised, but took it.

He popped the hatch and slipped in.

Aileen was on the bottom bunk. He knew she was alive because they had been monitoring her from above, but she didn't move now.

Looking close, one eye was swollen, like someone had punched her. Fur on her near arm had a cooked look to it, like someone had used a stun rod on her, grounding a tremendous amount of electricity into a Yithadreph.

Lazarus had no idea what that level of shock would do to a non-Human.

He reached out a tentative hand and touched the woman who had been his boss for a while.

"Aileen, it's Lazarus," he said.

She stirred, groaned, moved her head a little towards him.

"Wha?"

"It's Lazarus," he repeated.

Her good eye opened, found him, focused.

The woman surged up and wrapped her arms around his neck tight. He could feel her sobbing.

"They took Eha," she whispered. "I tried to stop them, but there were too many."

"I know," Lazarus wrapped his arms around the woman and held her. "I brought friends. We're going to get her back."

Something about his tone caused her to flinch, but he already knew what it was.

Humans, and their capability of mass violence. No other species moved as quickly to unmitigated force.

She leaned back finally and Lazarus got a good look at her face.

Battered. Badly. Someone using fists. Someone beating a woman much smaller than he was, as she was four foot six tall.

Someone Lazarus was going to kill slowly. Didn't have a name yet, but this was a missive he was willing to address as *Dear Occupant.*

He stood and got her upright.

Grace slipped into the cabin now and knelt.

"Aileen, this is Grace," Lazarus whispered. "She's a friend."

Aileen flinched at meeting a new Human, especially one with skin the color of aged oak, when Lazarus was pale with freckles, but she submitted to a quick inspection.

"On a Human, I'd say concussion and possibly a few fractures, but nothing bad," Grace said after a few moments, focusing her eyes on Aileen and raising a finger. "Follow my finger."

She moved it, and Lazarus could see the edges of a concussion. Not bad. Maybe the Yithadreph's head was just as hard as she was always saying.

"Now what?" Aileen asked.

"Now, we go up and rescue Eha," Lazarus replied coldly. "Whether those folks like it or not."

"He's going to kill her," Aileen said. "He had that look in his eyes, Ambassador or not."

"If he does, I'll let Addison burn this planet down," Lazarus replied, causing Grace's head to snap around.

"What?" she demanded in a tight voice.

"Eha's mate commands a warship unlike anything in the galaxy," Lazarus turned to her as she rose into his space. "It could kill Yisan. I'd help him."

Silence.

Long, painful, jagged.

Grace nodded. Maybe smiled grimly at some inside observation she wasn't willing to share.

They exited the cabin and closed the door.

"Now where?" Grace asked.

"Forward, up a deck," Aileen volunteered from her spot just behind Lazarus. "That's where Ardna was. He had guards outside the hatch and inside. Mostly inside."

"How many?" Grace asked.

"Six and two, I think," Aileen replied. "At least last time when I was up there."

"Good enough," Grace said.

Lazarus watched her turn to him with a smile and hand her stunner pistol to him. He took it blankly.

Watched her remove her drysuit top, unhook the front of her shirt that had been underneath, and pull it open, showing nothing but skin and breasts underneath.

He couldn't help but stare.

She chuckled.

"Yes, that will do," she said. "Lazarus, you stay close behind me and the others come along in the forward stairwell quietly."

She moved like a predator now. Forward up an empty corridor, so Lazarus presumed most of the crew on duty was either up on C-deck or down on A.

They made it to a forward stairwell. The rocking was getting a little worse now, but only noticeable because Lazarus was watching for it. Hopefully, nobody had noticed the three crew members removed from the situation.

Grace didn't have any weapons in her hands as they got to the top of the stairs. She pulled him close enough that he could feel the heat radiating off her skin.

"I'll approach and distract them," she whispered. "You keep anyone from coming up behind."

He had a hard time not staring at her chest, the way the shirt billowed open. He doubted Ardna's thugs would even try.

Lazarus settled for a silent nod.

Grace slid from the stairwell and stumbled across the hallway, using the wall to catch herself in an amazing imitation of staggering drunk.

"Whoopsie," she said in a voice like she was talking to herself a little too loud. "This way."

He watched her by sliding himself against the far edge. If he didn't stick his head out, the guards down there were as invisible as he was.

"Hey, boys," Grace slurred her. "I'm horny. Who wants to fool around?"

Lazarus remembered he was supposed to have her back, so he shifted to the other side and tracked the woman with his ears while his eyes and barrel quested aft.

"Who are you?" a male voice called in a low voice.

Quiet enough that nobody beyond a door would probably hear and want to interrupt a beautiful woman half-dressed and offering herself.

Lazarus heard a sound like Grace staggering into the wall again.

"Ardna brought me aboard as a surprise present fer someone," she mumbled loud enough. "Got a little drunk and tired of waiting. Need a man. You two man enough?"

That was cold. Challenging two thugs to take you at the same time? And drunk?

Lazarus smiled and listened. She was getting closer now.

"We're on duty, lady," another voice said, just as quietly. "What cabin are you in? We'll come for you in a while when the boss is done."

"You're cute," Grace said brightly. "So's your friend. I wanna ride you like a pony."

The next sound Lazarus heard only made sense if Grace punched one of them in the balls as hard as she could, pivoted, and drove a fist into the side of an unprepared head, into one of the soft spots. Then a couple of sharp kicks to settle the motion.

Followed only then by two bodies collapsing. Lazarus exploded into motion, checking aft quickly for movement and then turning forward in case Grace needed help.

She might need help dragging the two bodies out of her way. Not much more.

The smile on her face was calm glory. She gestured him closer.

"Let's move," Lazarus whispered into the stairwell.

"Was he at his desk?" Grace asked Aileen as they were all up front and set for violence.

Lazarus turned Oluchi to cover their rear now, and brought Xiuying and his repeat blaster up to the door.

"He was, last time," Aileen said. "Six men around him, four with guns and two have little wands that shock you."

Grace looked up at Lazarus and he nodded.

"There is a desk on the right as you enter," Grace said. "Two chairs on this side. Probably the six are in a circle five yards across, surrounding your friend and keeping her from moving."

"Capital," Xiuying smiled, patting his weapon. "I'll take care of them, then. You lot handle Ardna. Haven't see Khan yet, so hopefully he's in there waiting for me like a bride on her wedding night."

Xiuying turned and nodded at Aileen with a grim smile, and then a much happier one to Lazarus.

Again, Lazarus watched Grace defer to him. She didn't have to, but Eduardo had obviously told her to listen to the Rio Alliance officer. And she was probably a better shot than the rest of them.

"You take Ardna," Lazarus decided. "Xiuying softens up the room. Aileen, you stay off to one side. Oluchi, you've got the rear."

Aileen was pulling a pistol off one of the downed goons, but he wasn't going to argue with her right now. She'd been a good enough shot to nail him with a cargo harpoon, back on Zhoonarrim Station.

Lazarus stepped to the door. Double wide. Possibly locked. Not all that rugged, compared to some of the doors he'd had to go through in his time.

He turned to Xiuying.

"I'll knock it open, then you go to town," Lazarus said.

Any man who brought a weapon like that to raid a yacht had to know what he was doing. And the man had been starkly professional tonight.

Xiuying grinned.

Lazarus tested the lock, just to be sure. It seemed to turn, but he didn't want movement warning anyone inside, so he put his rifle across his back, grabbed both handles, and jammed them down, surging forward.

The doors parted like the Red Sea and Lazarus stumbled into the room. Rather than try to do anything, he just kept moving, shifting to his left as he saw all the people on his right before going to his knees.

That got him out of the way.

Xiuying wasn't a butcher. No, he was an artist. Holding a repeating blaster rifle. The sound was like a drunk woodpecker.

A woodpecker the size of a blue whale. The roar was deafening in the confined space.

And then silence. Just like that.

Not just like that. Strav Ardna had moved, possibly at the first sign of trouble. He was around the desk now, with a pistol in one hand and holding it against Eha's head, while his other had hold of her neck and kept her from moving away.

All the other goons were dead, smoking on the floor.

"I'll kill her," he screamed. "Don't you touch me or she's dead."

Lazarus started to stand, trying to find a way to get to the man before he could act. If Ardna pulled the trigger, she was dead and Strav Ardna would be in hell a second later, but he knew that. Wanted to survive.

Wanted a way out of this killzone he had brought them all into.

Their eyes met across the space. Strav Ardna didn't look Human right now. Rage and specism had taken over. Lazarus wondered how much longer Eha would have been alive, had they not intervened.

"You," Ardna sputtered as he focused on Lazarus.

His mouth opened to say something, but Grace shot

him, dead center of the face and snapped the skull back and up. The body fell bonelessly to the deck as the pistol clattered noisily.

Eha's scales were all as flared out as he'd ever seen a Churquen get. Lazarus stepped close enough for her to focus on him.

Light came back into them. She smiled.

Eha surprised him with a hug as fierce as Aileen's had been.

THIRTY-FIVE

EHA

SHE'D BEEN sure she was dead. Eha had done everything she could, used every evasion and misdirection she had ever learned in several decades of being a spy to confuse the Human.

In the end, it wouldn't have been enough. Or rather, it probably would have been, and he'd have turned to torture to get the details she wouldn't tell him otherwise.

But Strav Ardna was dead now.

She didn't understand any of it, still woozy from the brutality the other Humans had used on her and Aileen when the mighty furball decided to fight back.

Eha smiled at the memory of four Humans being necessary to stop one angry Yithadreph. And them armed with stun sticks of some sort.

She finally let go of Lazarus enough to stare at his face.

Frightened, but for her. Protective. Perhaps as much as Addison would have been, had he been here.

There were others. Aileen. Three Humans, one of which looked female, since she was smaller than the other two and built more like Aileen. Breasts. Curves.

There was still an edge of terrible lethality about the woman.

Her skin was a brown darker than umber, so radically different from the freckled paleness of Lazarus. For any race other than Humans she would have guessed the woman to be a different species, but she already knew Humans showed more genetic diversity than any other species in space. One of the men looked close enough to Lazarus to be of the same subspecies, but the other had skin nearly golden, with radically different bones in the face and eye sockets not nearly as round.

So interesting.

"Eha, these are my friends," Lazarus said, gesturing to them. "You remember Oluchi Pryce. This is Grace Savidge and Xiuying Bălan. You're safe now."

"Thank you," she breathed, including Aileen in her look.

Then she studied the rest of the room. Felt her scales flare out all the way again.

Seven dead Humans. Strav Ardna and six guards. Gone so fast it was still a blur and a roar to her.

Eha turned to the side, keeping one arm around Lazarus for strength, both physical and moral. She'd imagined Human violence. Dreamed terrible nightmares about it.

She'd dreamed too small.

Lazarus turned to the Human woman, seeming to concede to her control of the situation. Eha wondered who the woman was.

Grace Savidge pulled out a hand communicator and pressed a button. Put it to her ear. Grimaced.

"It's done," she said simply. "Ruthlessly."

She listened, turning to watch the two alien women and the one Eha supposed could be classified as an alien man. Human friends had been a theoretical thing.

Now, she had one. At least one, from the welcoming looks on the others.

Grace turned to Lazarus with the device still to her ear.

"What about innocents?" she asked.

"There aren't any on this ship." Oluchi Pryce stepped closer.

He still looked a little older than Lazarus. A shade taller, but leaner. Prettier, if she had to put a word to it, but she wasn't sure how Human males would react to the term, if they were anything at all like Churquen.

"Pryce?" Grace turned to the newcomer.

"Ardna was capable of monitoring and recording cabins I was assured were utterly private when I was last aboard," Oluchi Pryce said. "So he's probably blackmailing a few people. Or was. That means the crew is complicit. And the thugs who came at us in the car with guns and threats don't get to claim innocence now. I'm with Lazarus. They're bullies who met a bigger fist."

"Eduardo?" Grace said into the comm.

Eha had no idea who she was talking to, but it appeared to be someone important. Her brain was still a little wobbly from the physical abuse.

"He recommends a terrible accident," Grace said aloud. "With no survivors."

"Good enough," Lazarus said. "We can swim away."

"I can't," Eha spoke up. "Churquen sink really well."

Aileen stepped close.

"I'll keep you safe, Eha," she murmured.

Lazarus turned to the males.

"Oluchi, is there another diving helmet we can steal?" he asked. "The storm's too big for surface swimming."

The man thought for a moment.

"Yes, near the fantail."

"Good, you and Xiuying go get it and we'll meet you there," Lazarus said. "Kill anyone you encounter."

"And you?" Xiuying asked.

"Grace and I will sabotage the engines to cause an explosion and fire," he said. "That will destroy most of the evidence, and it's not like Yisan has much of a police force to investigate it afterwards. We'll be gone quickly from this planet anyway and only us and Eduardo will know the truth."

Lazarus turned within her arm to study her.

"Eha, I'm sorry," he said simply. "For all of this. Hopefully, you and Addison will be mollified by such an offering. You and Aileen go with Oluchi, and we'll be up shortly."

Eha leaned close enough to rest her cheek on his shoulder, just happy to be alive. Lazarus was right, though. Addison would be furious, so they might have to skip over some of the details. She could only imagine what he might have done had she died here.

It was wonderful, having such a mate that he might consider rising to the Human level when it came to violence, but counter-productive, if they wished Human assistance overthrowing the Innruld.

Oluchi stepped closer now and smiled diffidently.

"Are you ready?" he asked, holding out a hand like a gentlemen biped helping a lady into a vehicle.

She took it, understanding the cultural translation and accepting him. Her own wits and reflexes felt like she was wrapped in cotton batting as everything was just slightly the wrong color.

She followed the smaller Human past the bodies and into the corridor. Up a spiraling staircase that was actually probably easier for her to use than Humans, although Aileen's quiet grumbles weren't silent.

The vessel felt like it was rocking harder than it had earlier. Perhaps a storm was rising outside.

Eha had spent most of her adult life on space stations, rather than the surface of planets. The very concept of a boat floating on a large body of water was so alien and frightening to the Churquen that she had wondered if Ardna had done this to her on purpose, but none of the Humans seemed fazed by it. Yithadreph were already a semi-aquatic species.

The group emerged onto the main deck she remembered, her vision finally settling and growing crisper as the various shocks began to wear off. The space looked like a lounge, with a bar to one side and bench couches with pillows where Humans might enjoy relaxing.

Nothing for her to settle in a good coil.

She watched water actually fall from the sky outside a window.

Oluchi opened what she had thought was a closet and pulled out a helmet for a Human. She would have said a helmet for a space suit, but this ship didn't fly.

Diving helmet. For Humans to swim beneath the water.

What a terrifying concept.

"May I?" he asked as he stepped close.

Aileen and the other man, Xiuying, were watching both ways with guns, so Eha tried to relax.

She nodded and watched Oluchi step close and make adjustments to the thing in his hands. It split open in a ring at the bottom, and he reached around to rest it on her neck.

"This is designed for Human skin, so it will inflate enough to press and hold," he said, studying her closely. "I have no idea how it will work on scales, so I'm going to set it to maintain positive pressure, meaning it will leak bubbles around you constantly, but that should keep water out, and there is enough power for the gills to run for days, even doing this."

Gills? Ah, artificial gills pulling oxygen out of the water for a Human to breathe.

Bizarre.

Still, it might be possible to adapt such a thing for a Churquen. She would need fins like her aquatic cousins if she chose to do this again, but she suspected that Humans could adapt something there as well.

The helmet ring closed around her neck and inflated. She had to hold herself still, as it felt like hands started to choke her.

"Are you okay?" Oluchi asked, staring at her from close.

"Yes," she lied.

Mostly lied. This was what was necessary to get her off the boat and apparently make the ensuing event look like an accident. She would slither backwards across hot coals if that was what it took.

The back of the helmet was designed for Humans, of course. Their necks didn't turn or flex like hers, so she would need to remain more still when they went into the water.

Into an ocean. During a storm.

She could see more water falling from the sky. Actual rain. And wind. The boat was turned into the storm, near as she could tell, but growing more wobbly every minute.

Oluchi pulled a back piece up and it clicked. She was half blind.

He smiled at her anyway.

"My eyes are more centered than yours," he said with a friendly nod. "When we commission a version for you, it will have more glass."

Like she was going to turn into an adventurer and swim in open water?

Eha reconsidered. She might. Already, she had done a score of crazy things, starting with fleeing the authorities at Zhoonarrim Station aboard *Shiva Zephyr Glaive.*

What was one more?

Oluchi took her hand and guided it to her right temple. Humans were right-hand dominant, for the most part.

"This button closes the faceshield," he said. "Tap it when you're ready."

Eha took a breath and pressed. Three plates snapped out and locked together, both bottom sides and down from the top. The seam where they met was almost invisible. Soft lights came on inside the helmet and she felt it blow air into her face.

Oluchi grabbed his own helmet and donned it while she watched. Weirdly, he touched the flat parts of his window to hers.

"Can you hear me?" he asked.

Ah, useful. Vibrations passed through both systems if you didn't have radios. Space suits worked in a similar manner, but she'd never imagined space-exploring underwater.

At least until tonight.

"I can," Eha answered, watching him smile again.

For a Human she had known less than a day, he seemed like he was trying his damnedest to help. As were the others.

Lazarus had said that there would be Humans on her side. She hadn't really believed it until now. The last several hours had left a sour taste in her mouth.

Oluchi stepped back and turned to the others, popping open his faceplate. Eha did the same.

"There's a sled in the water nearby," he announced. "I'm going to go try to recover it while you two keep watch for the others."

Xiuying nodded, so Eha watched the man step out onto the rear deck of the vessel and felt the wind howl in through the open hatch. The open door had let in a tremendous wind and splattered rain on things. It would be ugly out there.

Then she would be going into water. How fast would she sink?

"You'll be fine," Aileen was suddenly close and holding her hand.

Eha wished she could agree, as she watched the Human close up his faceplate and dive headlong off the rear of the boat, disappearing from sight.

THIRTY-SIX
OLUCHI

THERE WAS something to be said about casting loose from the man he'd been yesterday.

Oluchi knifed into the water like all the pretty women were watching from the flying bridge. Grace had set the sled to station-keeping on the ship, but the rain was bad enough he couldn't see it from the deck.

Just the endless gloom of the ocean depths.

Right about now, he wished he had a knife, in case something came up from below for a nibble, but wishes weren't fishes, so he turned and looked back up at the surface.

There.

Marker lights outlining the device at a depth of about fifteen feet, level with the bottom of the hull like a mat of seaweed.

Oluchi swam up to the device and found the controls. He'd used something similar, and they were all designed to be used by tourists with a modicum of training, so getting it to turn and rise to the surface wasn't that impossible.

Hopefully, the sea wasn't so cold that Eha would be

unable to swim or hold on. Aileen had fur and hopefully a layer of insulation, since she looked like an otter already, and seemed fine with water.

There were no drysuits for a Churquen. He doubted enough of them might take up such a daredevil hobby, if they were that afraid of water, but he made a note to investigate what sorts of things Humans might manufacture for all their new alien friends. He couldn't make it, but if he had the inside track, he could make sure Eduardo's friends could before anyone else, and then get cut in for a slice or a license.

That was probably why Eduardo really wanted him involved. After all, if he was going to be a fixer he really need to think like a pimp. And most of his clients would probably be legitimate businesspeople. If he had to finally grow up and rely purely on his wits instead of just his looks, then that might be an excellent place to carve out his next niche.

Especially as the aliens would eventually want to return home, hopefully with a list of needs that the traders of Yisan —*the surviving traders*—could deliver.

Oluchi surfaced with the sled not far from the rear of the boat, on the side near the ladder. Heads appeared above him and he saw both Aileen and Lazarus looking down, so he waved.

Aileen surprised him by diving immediately into the water, turning, and popping up almost in his hip pocket. Apparently, Yithadreph enjoyed water.

Otter, right.

The storm was starting to get ugly, so Oluchi was spending most of his attention keeping the sled from being pushed away as *Cardinal* sat still in the surf. Grace dove next, popping up on his other side, from Aileen. Oluchi let go of the controls and shifted out of her way, on the assumption she was a better driver than he was, and knew where she needed to go next.

Instead, he focused his attention on the top of the ladder. Churquen could not use a Human ladder. He presumed she might prefer an old-fashioned brass pole like fire stations had in all the ancient classics. And she didn't have the upper body strength of a Human, so she was just holding on to one of Lazarus's hands with both of hers.

The man was stronger than he looked. Or angrier. Never discount that option. He lowered Eha bodily until Oluchi could grab hold of her tail and sort of guide her over to the sled. Grace assisted by driving them right up to the point that Aileen was using her spare hand to keep the sled from banging too hard on the hull.

Eha's mask was closed, but she was on the edge of panic, so Oluchi just wrapped an arm all the way around her and then grabbed hold of the sled. After a moment, she realized what he was doing and wrapped her coil around his legs.

He nearly lost his own grip in surprise, but then laughed at himself. Of course, that would be how a Churquen held on.

Lazarus followed her down the ladder, with a bag over his shoulder presumably holding the blaster pistols, possibly including the one he had abandoned earlier when he was fitting Eha.

Xiuying appeared last, breaking his gun down into parts and stuffing them into a bag he had stolen from the same closet as Eha's helmet. Rather than jump, he walked slowly backwards down the ladder and sort of fell into the water, barely arm's reach from the sled.

Once Xiuying grabbed on, Grace backed them away, letting the tide carry them backwards. She turned to the left and opened the throttle. Oluchi slid his hands as close together around Eha's chest as he could while holding on to the sled, thankful that she didn't have actual breasts he might be touching right now. Although he supposed that might be acceptable, given the alternatives.

She was holding on to both him and the sled for dear life. He could live with the bruises she was going to leave everywhere with her coils.

Grace took them down about fifteen feet. The surf above was lashing and churning, but the waters down here were calmer. Oluchi glanced back and saw the lights of *Cardinal* receding into nothingness as they got far enough away from the boat.

He heard the first explosion. Felt it in his rib cage. It wasn't all that big, but the water transmitted the sound perfectly. They were too far away to see the boat, but he heard a long series of popping sounds after that. More explosions, but smaller.

Finally, Grace maneuvered them to the surface, an octopus with all manner of strange legs trailing off the sled. Lights appeared above them and Oluchi recognized the van that had brought them out originally, with something like a cargo net trailing out the open door.

Lazarus went up first, followed by Xiuying. Nobody had said anything to Oluchi, so he concentrated on Eha, glancing back over his shoulder when breaks in the waves and rain let him see a bonfire in the distance.

Cardinal, burning.

Terrible, terrible accident.

Honest.

A crane arm came out and a line dropped. It had a hook on the end that Grace secured to the top of the sled and then she motioned for him to move himself and Eha to the net.

She didn't want to let go of the sled. He couldn't really blame her.

Instead, he turned her to face him, and saw how big her eyes had gotten.

"Eha, we need to climb into the vehicle now," he yelled as he touched faceplates with her. "You're safe, and now we can get out of the water. You have to trust me. We'll take care of you."

Something got through to her. He felt the death grip slacken some around his thighs. She turned inside his arms and wrapped her own arms around his neck, to go with her coil around his legs.

At least they both had helmets, because as soon as he let go, they slid under water, and she started to squeeze painfully. Strong arms grabbed his shoulder and pulled him back up before he got too far down.

Grace. And Aileen a moment later.

Oluchi was just a post that Eha was holding, as the other two women got him to the net. He grabbed it himself and tried to pull, but they weighed too much combined.

Instead, more hands grabbed him. He looked up and both Lazarus and Xiuying had hooked themselves to the vehicle, laid out flat on their stomachs, and were pulling him up with just their arms.

Once they got high enough, Eha started to breathe again. He could feel her heart pounding against his chest, but she looked around as Oluchi got one of his feet onto the cargo net and could push.

Eha found her own grip, spun away from him, and flowed uphill like a dot of mercury into the rear of the vehicle. Oluchi joined her a moment later. She handed him a second towel and he dried the outside of his suit off rather than trying to explain drysuits to the woman.

She was already cocooned and shivering, so he handed his towel to Aileen and sat next to Eha. She leaned against him and he sort of pulled her onto his lap, as much as he could, and let her draw strength from contact. It worked with Human women. Hopefully, it would work with aliens as well.

Grace was in just after Aileen, and the sled was pulled up by the winch and stood upright as the hatch closed and the sounds of the storm receded.

"Let's go," Grace called to the driver whose name he didn't know, and Oluchi felt the van turn away from the storm and race away towards shore.

Eha just sat, wrapped around him as she shivered.

Oluchi smiled. Could he call himself a fixer now? He'd solved his first problem, but looking around he knew that there would be more.

THIRTY-SEVEN
LAZARUS

LAZARUS HAD MOVED QUICKLY from the explosion and fire that was destroying Ardna's yacht out beyond the harbor. This wasn't a place where police carefully investigated things and possibly came to arrest him and his compatriots for their crimes, but news would get out quickly enough. The driver he didn't know might talk. Or Eduardo might. Hell, the strangers in the back of the van with him probably couldn't all keep their mouths shut about what they'd done.

He needed to be gone off the planet before first light if he could.

That might not be possible, as Eha seemed to be in shock, but Grace took another look at her and pronounced her fit. The NavCrawler Cormac might be the only person truly capable of knowing about Aileen, but she seemed to be in good enough shape. Nothing a long sleep and some food wouldn't cure, at least to hear her talk.

Still, Lazarus wanted to get back to the others, to his friends, as soon as possible.

His other friends. He had made a few here, else they

wouldn't have been willing to do what they'd just done, even with the possibility of trade being dangled in front of them.

The van was approaching the starport now over roads, rather than flying high. Nobody was allowed any elevation around the starport, so that ships taking off and landing didn't have to worry. Everyone on the ground stayed low and drove on roads, hovering or not.

Grace turned to him now and studied his face. Neither of them were wearing drysuits now, back in normal clothing, so they might be two strangers who'd met at a bus stop. She didn't speak, so he remained silent until he knew what was going through her mind.

"You aren't staying, are you?" she finally asked.

Lazarus nodded, a little surprised that she'd been able to read that from his face, but he supposed he wasn't hiding it all that much.

"Will you return?" she continued.

Lazarus shrugged, unwilling to commit to words right now. Addison would certainly probably demand to return, but his intentions wouldn't be polite. Hopefully, with Ardna and his people dead, Wolcott would be willing to let that one go.

Eha was safe.

Lazarus would have destroyed the place himself if something had happened to her.

"Eduardo instructed me to protect you," Grace said with a wry, sideways kind of smile. "I can't do that if you leave. I'd like to come along, if I could."

Lazarus blinked. Blinked again. It didn't help.

Words failed when he opened his mouth. Right now, Grace Savidge didn't look like someone who was just coming along because she had been ordered to by her boss.

No, her eyes held ulterior motives. Not all that ulterior,

and probably not what Eduardo Martìnez had intended, having only known him for a day. The man wasn't that good at identifying the weaknesses of a stranger like Lazarus, was he?

"It will be a while," Lazarus managed to sputter. "Brasilia, and I'm not sure how long we'll be there. Then hopefully returning the others home. Not sure when we'll see Yisan again."

"You obviously need help staying out of trouble," Grace smiled at him, drawing his own smile to the surface.

"Quite possibly," Lazarus said, "if the last year is any indication. Are you sure?"

She shifted in such a way that she could touch the tip of his nose with hers.

"Pretty sure," she murmured.

Lazarus was glad she didn't try to kiss him right now, but didn't think that was very far off. At least he was single, if it came to that.

"He's going to need lots of help staying out of trouble," Aileen popped up and broke Grace's spell as everyone laughed. "I can speak to that."

Lazarus looked around at the others.

"I would also travel with you, if I may," Oluchi said, with Eha still mostly wrapped around him.

Her scales looked better. Almost flat. Her eyes, turning this way, were almost back to normal.

Lazarus considered the former gigolo and playboy gambler. Oluchi Pryce would be a professional representative for Eduardo, which would be useful if Grace had personal reasons in coming. And the man had transformed from who he'd been when he walked up and joined them for tea. Had it only been sixteen hours ago?

But he had changed. That much was obvious, and Lazarus was used to judging men and women to see who was ready and capable of promotion, when several crew members were all vying for only one open slot.

Still, he looked at Eha. She nodded and smiled a tiny smile at him.

"You need a killer, mate?" Xiuying asked. "Yisan's been okay but with Khan dead it's gonna get kinda boring. And this is the most fun I've had in years."

"We're going back to the Rio Alliance," Lazarus reminded them, looking at each face in sequence. "Anybody got active warrants for their arrest, when we get to a civilized planet?"

He nearly laughed when each of them had to stop and think about that for a moment before deciding they were probably safe.

An assassin, a killer, and a gambler. Sounded like the beginning of a bad joke, but he'd take them.

It would be interesting when they met the rest of the crew.

THIRTY-EIGHT

EHA

EHA LET the solidity of the pincke, the tiny cargo shuttle that had brought them Yisan, give her strength. The last day had been a nightmare made flesh, but hopefully they were past everything.

Oluchi was talking to Eduardo Martìnez on a pocket comm as Lazarus and the dark-skinned woman did their preflight. Aileen was instructing the other Human, Xiuying, where to store weapons, as most of the gear had remained in the van when it departed.

"What about clothing and personal effects?" Oluchi looked up and turned his head both ways.

"Clothing we can handle at the ship," Lazarus looked back over his shoulder with a smile Eha could only classify as cruel, but he also hadn't told them the truth about *Ajax* yet.

That it had uniforms for every size and shape of Human, plus a Necherle tailor who'd probably look on the whole affair as an exciting challenge.

"And the rest?" Oluchi asked.

"We'll be to Brasilia fast enough," the man said cryptically.

Eha still hadn't wrapped her coils around the star drives that Humans used. Open a hole in space and step immediately through it, rather than trans-drives that might take days to get even somewhere close.

On top of everything else, that would give Humans an unmatchable edge in exploration. And warfare, if it came to that. Nothing the Innruld could do would let them catch a Human ship.

"Good enough," Oluchi apparently relayed from the Human trader. "He says good luck and Godspeed."

Eha agreed with that sentiment. Escape Yisan ahead of any vendettas related to killing a powerful merchant and decapitating his organization suddenly. Get to a place where there were hopefully rules around behavior and she could go back to being an Ambassador, rather than a prisoner.

Oluchi flipped down a seat close by, but not next to her. His eyes studied her whole form, but it had the feel of making sure she was okay, rather than Ardna's loathing or another man seeing her as a strange sex object.

A friend. One she had known for less than a day, but concerned about her a person.

Humans were weird.

But hadn't Lazarus been equally accepted by Addison's crew?

A stranger in trouble, and the Humans leapt to her rescue.

"Everybody grab seats and strap yourselves in," Lazarus called. "We have clearance to launch."

Aileen ended up next to her, opposite Oluchi, while Xiuying sat down across the bay. The seatbelts for Humans didn't fit her all that well, but she'd made do on the flight here. She would make do on the way back to *Ajax*.

The craft lifted a little and taxied over to the launch zone. In a way, it was similar to exiting a station bay into the tunnel that would take you out into deep space, in preparation for the trans-drives engaging.

Here, the ship was headed up for deep space. Eha kept herself coiled around the seat and held on when gravity wanted to drag her to the right. Stations in orbit were so much more efficient, for exactly this reason, but she couldn't really argue with the success of the Humans, doing it their own way.

The pressure on her relented after about forty-five minutes. Over shoulders up front, she could see darkness and stars as they cleared the atmosphere and began crossing deep space.

Conversation hadn't been impossible under the pressure of launch, but difficult enough that Aileen had settled for occasionally squeezing her hand silently.

Eha still didn't feel like chatting, but was far too polite to actually say anything. Instead, she just closed her eyes and leaned back, letting the absence of gravity loosen all the kinks that had worked themselves into her body, both from stress as well as bruises.

"We are ready for star drives," Lazarus said simply.

For a moment, Eha felt the entire universe blink, too fast to notice except in retrospect.

But that was the Human technology. Blink, and they're gone.

"*Ajax*, this is Lazarus," he said. "Reply on this channel."

They waited. It might take a while, as Addison and his crew would have no idea when the pincke would be returning, so they might be off having their own adventures with the ship.

She would ask how much trouble someone could get into in three days, but she had a strong answer to that silliness, so she kept her humor to herself.

"Now what?" Grace asked, loud enough for the people in

the cargo bay to also hear.

"Now, we wait," Lazarus replied simply. "We're close enough to the right coordinates, but didn't specify a tighter rendezvous than that. They might be anywhere within a few light-hours right now, so we probably have some time if people want to unfold the hammocks and take a nap."

Eha was off the chair, holding on with only the tip of her tail, before anybody else could even move, but they had to let go and fly, even in a shuttle this small. She could just stand on the Churquen equivalent of tiptoes and open the cabinet she wanted.

It looked like a piece of cloth, but that was deceiving as she pulled herself back to a hook and attached it. Across the way, she hooked the other side and just flowed right up into the cargo net in a single motion.

Oluchi looked at her with surprise before he laughed. He grabbed another one and hooked it more slowly, having to work carefully while she watched.

Still, this was not his first attempt, as he got the hammock hung and pulled himself in then latched the front closed.

"Who has watch?" Aileen asked, forever on duty on a ship, worried about cargo, even the organic kind.

"You sleep," Lazarus said. "I'm too keyed up and you need the rest."

Aileen didn't argue, but Eha could see the tiredness around the man's edges. He'd been up all night, and engaged in a rescue, but nobody had used physical brutality on him at any point.

Grace, the Human woman, remained in station with him, so they would be able to watch for *Ajax*.

Eha didn't think she'd be calm enough to actually fall asleep as she closed her eyes.

She was wrong.

THIRTY-NINE

LAZARUS

LAZARUS WATCHED the woman next to him as everyone else settled in for something like a nap. Meditation. Something. Apparently Churquen snored, but he'd once had a cat that was louder, except when the little tom started squeaking.

They were as alone as they would likely get, before Grace started to learn his real secrets. It would be interesting to see her response at that point.

"What should I prepare for?" she asked in a voice a trace above a whisper.

Lazarus thought about it for a moment.

"We're none of us what we appear," he replied, staring right at her and daring the woman to flinch. Or something.

"You're Rio Alliance Navy," she said simply, surprising him. "I've been around enough of you people to see the habits. What was the secret mission you were on?"

Lazarus remembered to pick his jaw up off the deck after a moment.

Grace smiled at him knowingly.

"Technically, I can't tell you," he said.

"That's fine," she started to say, but he overrode her and continued, regardless of how poor manners it might be.

"However, you'll learn more than you should as soon as Addison gets here, so you might as well be prepared," Lazarus said. "The vessel is named *Ajax*."

"That's an odd name for an alien craft, even if they do speak our tongue," Grace scowled at him.

"It's not alien," Lazarus smiled. "*Ajax* is Rio Alliance Navy."

"But you said the alien was in command," Grace's fierceness turned up a notch. "Eha's mate."

"I left Addison Wolcott in charge when I went to Yisan," Lazarus corrected her. "It's an experimental craft, designed for a small crew to operate, at least in the circumstances we're using it."

"How could a ship that small have enough firepower to annihilate Yisan then, or at least Tershuvi Port?"

"It's not small, Grace," he smiled. "*Ajax* is a warship. My ship."

It was her turn to pick up her jaw. She repeated the words silently, not even breathing.

"I designed the vessel," Lazarus continued. "Built it around an experimental weapon, and packed it full of bleeding edge technology. The goal was to build something that could defeat Westphalia."

"But aliens?" she gulped.

"Accident," he said grimly. "Our first cruise dropped us into a Westphalian GunWall ambush. I was fighting for my life before I knew what happened. The rest of my crew abandoned ship and I decided to destroy the craft. In that, I failed, had some wild adventures I'll tell you about another time, then eventually recruited the crew of Addison Wolcott's tramp freighter to help me fly *Ajax*. They've been training aboard her for about a month now."

"The aliens have the ship?" Grace gasped.

"I trust them more than I trust anyone else right now, Grace," he said perhaps a shade sharper than he originally intended. "There's a spy somewhere in the Rio Alliance who told Westphalia where to find me. That person is still there. Strav Ardna tried to kill one of my friends. Not an alien I was transporting home to my superiors. My *friend*."

She fell silent, studying his face for some sign he wasn't sure of.

Something.

"At some point, someone's going to address you by some other name than Lazarus, aren't they?" Grace asked finally.

Maybe there was a smile there. Maybe not. Hard to tell.

"They will," Lazarus replied, "but I'm not him anymore. I'm not really sure I remember him, truth be told."

"What will your papers say, if they have to reissue them after the emergency?"

"Francisco Luiz Oliveira," he replied evenly. "*Capitão De Mar E Guerra*. My friends used to call me *Pancho*."

"I think I prefer Lazarus," Grace said, finally smiling a little.

"Me, too," he grinned back, shrugging. "It's been a weird year."

"So what will you tell the fussy, old admirals, when you show up again with aliens and criminals?" her smile grew as she asked.

"The galaxy has changed," Lazarus said. "It's bigger than anyone imagined, and we're in a position to maybe do something grand and good with it. They'll just have to deal with all the strangers I picked up along the way if they want my help."

"Your help?"

"I'm the only Human who knows where the others came from," he smiled like a shark now. "If you want those coordinates, you'll have to deal with me. Or one of my friends."

"I'm pretty sure that's Pryce's job," she leaned a little closer and put a hand on his arm. "I'm supposed to keep you safe."

"That means assassins, Grace," he said simply.

"Other assassins, Lazarus," her smile turned grim, but it was still warm. "Eduardo instructed me to help you and protect you. And you might be the most important Human in space right now, so I better do a good job."

Somehow, they were both leaning forward, talking in barely a whisper now. Lazarus wondered what her kiss would taste like, but wasn't sure it was safe to know.

Not all of her motives were ulterior, but there would be some he might not find out about until it was too late. Dangerous, dangerous woman.

But he already knew that.

Attractive, if you liked them athletic and slim, rather than curvy and overdeveloped.

Lethal, in good ways as well as bad.

Lazarus was rescued by the sensor board beeping madly on the console between them. He reached down and checked the readings as an excuse not to kiss this eminently kissable woman, when it might be a trap.

But weren't all women traps? Some of them you just didn't necessarily want to escape from.

Lazarus looked back up at Grace and smiled as he killed the alarm and opened the comm.

"You're back earlier than we expected," Addison's voice came over the system and filled the whole space of the pincke. "Is everything okay?"

"We ran into some trouble on Yisan, Addison," Lazarus replied. "But I was able to recruit some more friends, some

Human ones, and we got everything sorted out. Where are you?"

"Looking at my boards, Kuei dropped us out of jump almost behind you," Addison called. "Relative motion almost zero, except for some drift from solar wind differentials between here and there. Company, you said?"

"Correct," Lazarus smiled. "Grace Savidge, Oluchi Pryce, and Xiuying Bălan. They're aboard the pincke and will be coming to Brasilia with us. The password is Zhoonarrim."

"Understood, Lazarus," Addison said carefully. "See you shortly."

They had set up a series of code words, if something had gone wrong and they needed to communicate. Or if Wybert needed to practice his weapons on the pincke. Blowing Lazarus to hell and returning to liberate Innruld Space themselves was a possibility not all that far down the list.

He was just glad it was unnecessary.

Lazarus cut the line and looked over at Grace, utterly silent through the whole exchange.

"Friends?" she asked quietly, an unsure smile on her face.

Ulterior motives.

"At least," he replied, smiling some. "All hands, brace for maneuvers."

He glanced back and saw eyes staring at him from the partial darkness of the cargo bay, so he brought the lights back up and busied his hands on the controls.

The pincke rotated slowly in place on all three axes, and Grace gasped out loud when the windshield showed *Ajax* coming into view.

"That thing's huge!" she said, turning a concerned face to him.

"Light Starcruiser," he replied. "It was the smallest I could build it, to fit the primary weapons system."

"The one that could destroy Tershuvi Port?"

"That one," he nodded.

"What will you do with it?" her face softened into something that wasn't just curiosity, but also included it.

"Teach Westphalia some manners," Lazarus said. "Then go help my friends."

"Problems in alien space?" Grace's eyes narrowed.

Rather than answer, Lazarus just nodded and engaged the engines to start them forward.

"Will we need to help them, after we help you?" Grace asked.

He liked the assumption the woman made that she'd still be involved. And that his Rio Alliance bosses would let him or her do that.

Of course, he might not give them the option to say no. He didn't know who the spy was that had nearly gotten him killed, so Lazarus of Bethany was going to be rather a bit more reticent and circumspect than *Pancho* Oliveira had ever been.

"Perhaps," he temporized.

"It won't be allowed?"

From the look on her face, she was guessing, but it was an easy guess.

"They might try to stop me," Lazarus replied. "But I'm already a pirate in Innruld Space."

FORTY

OLUCHI

OLUCHI HAD NEVER SERVED in anything like a formal military, so he didn't really understand the oohs and ahs from the others as the ship filled more and more of the front window, finally turning into a wall with a window, the dock that they were flying into.

Apparently, the thing was huge, compared to other Rio ships. He wasn't even remotely an expert, having spent his time on comparatively tiny tramp freighters or semi-luxury liners, plying his various trades.

Xiuying was impressed. That told Oluchi enough to listen to the man. Neither of the other two recognized the design of the vessel, but it was friendly and would be his chariot to the heart of the Rio Alliance and all the things Eduardo would be expecting of him there.

They flew into a bay and landed on magnets, thumping with a jar transmitted all the way up his spine. A moment later, gravity was extended to the ship, bringing a solid down to his sensibilities. The hull hummed, which he presumed were the bay doors closing. A hiss as atmosphere flooded the chamber.

Lazarus stood as everything was powered down.

"My friends, welcome aboard the Rio Alliance warship *Ajax*," he said simply. "I figured I should warn you up front that the four of us are the only Humans aboard at present, with my other friends providing the entirety of the current crew, at least until we get home and determine our next steps."

No Humans aboard? None?

Coupled with the immense size of the ship, Oluchi finally understood now the sorts of risk that Yisan hadn't been aware they faced. An alien warship might indeed have taken offense at Eha's kidnapping and decided to punish all Humans.

Would that have led to a war? Another war?

Oluchi couldn't see Westphalia ever making common cause with non-Humans, for anything longer than catching the Rio Alliance in a pincer and destroying it.

He would need to make sure that Yisan wasn't collateral damage, in ways Eduardo probably didn't imagine, at least outside of his nightmares.

"Now what?" Oluchi spoke up, as it became clear that Lazarus was waiting for someone to speak.

"Now, we board the ship, get all of you settled, and prepare to head inward," Lazarus said.

Oluchi watched him key the big rear hatch open when the lights turned green, indicating a safe atmosphere, and the panel lowered into a ramp.

Just because, Oluchi offered Eha his arm. She took it with a jolt of surprise followed by a wry smile. Aileen harrumphed a moment later, so he grinned at her and offered his other arm.

What better way to board a strange ship than with a woman on each arm?

Xiuying rolled his eyes with a grin and shook his head, which just made it better.

Lazarus walked down the ramp first, with Grace close but not that close. Awkwardly a step farther away from the man than her walk might have suggested, like she wanted to be on his arm, but they hadn't worked that much out yet.

He'd seen enough signs to understand.

Oluchi followed, escorting the ladies down onto the deck, with Xiuying bringing up the rear noisily. Much louder than he'd walked on the decks of *Cardinal,* so Oluchi supposed he was making a statement.

Or setting false expectations about how quietly the man could move, if he needed to later.

Lazarus led them to an airlock. Again, a standard, Human design three times as deep as a standard lift like you might find in a luxury hotel. Everyone fit, with a bit of adjusting, since the Humans had never had to worry about stepping on a tail or tripping over one before now.

The door to the bay closed and the inner one opened.

Oluchi managed to keep the shock off his face, he hoped. A lifetime of poker and trysts probably helped.

Another Churquen awaited them in a larger chamber beyond. Male, just because Oluchi could see the gender differences now. That would be Addison Wolcott, Eha's mate.

And the current commander of the ship.

Next to Wolcott was a…

Thing. Oluchi didn't have a better term to describe it.

Two gray disks, each about six inches thick, sandwiched together around a central hub that was about eighteen inches wide and covered with a heavy hide that vaguely reminded him of an elephant. The whole creature was about four feet tall, with the central part maybe three feet in diameter, so the creature could roll with clearance.

The central part had either an eye, or what looked like a mouth, interspersed all around the circumference. Two spindly arms emerged from the axle, ending in six-finger claws that reminded him of the game machine where you tried to pull a prize up and transport it to the little well where it could be retrieved. Most of them were scams, but the claws were similar.

At least one of the eyes was staring at him.

Maybe.

Lazarus emerged, walking up to Wolcott as the rest of them followed. Eha dropped his arm and surged into Wolcott's, tangling like a pair of bungee cords left overnight in a drawer.

Other aliens surrounded them as Aileen stepped a little farther away from him. They were all tiny, at least compared to Humans. Aileen was roughly in the middle, when he had unconsciously been expecting her to be small.

Were Humans just that big, compared to the rest of the galaxy?

One of the creatures was a giant spider, reared back almost like a dog sitting on its hind legs, except that doing so freed up the creature's hands and arms to be crossed across its thorax. Fine black hairs, interspersed with several other colors in such a way that it was almost a glowing rainbow, or would be when the lighting was just right.

A giant, tan, glider squirrel watched, stepping close to Aileen for a hug, those eyes never leaving him, but the face not snarling.

Lazarus had warned them all about Wybert of Capantzina, but the man seemed mostly relaxed. It helped that none of the travelers were currently armed, with all the blasters and such stored aboard the pincke for transit.

Wybert was armed rather more heavily than was necessary.

The creature was turquoise, more or less. He had an

upright torso with two pairs of arms, top and bottom, and head atop that with five eyes, two antennae, and a mouth of nightmares, with four finger-like appendages ending in spike-like claws for drawing food in.

On each hip, if you could call them hips, Wybert had a holster with a Manticore pistol in them, rather like a gunslinger. Across his chest and the top of his abdomen, Oluchi could see a semi-rigid armor like a breastplate in several pieces.

Ten legs all ended in feet like the spider's, if he had to compare them to anything.

And the top arms were holding a long spear with a metal tip over a foot long and as wide as his palm.

Wybert wasn't threatening anyone, but Lazarus had warned them that the man could be a bit high-strung, whatever that meant.

Once Eha stopped kissing Wolcott, Lazarus gestured to the rest of them.

"Addison, my new friends," he said. "Grace, Xiuying, and Oluchi. Permission to come aboard?"

"Granted," the Churquen male said. "Welcome home. Things did not go well?"

Eha had more or less untangled herself and drifted over to one side, putting her closer to Oluchi than the rest of the Humans, but still holding an arm around Wolcott's waist, just as he had around hers. The last foot or so of their tales were intertwined.

"We ran into someone with Westphalian sensibilities," Lazarus said carefully, obviously not wanting to set Wolcott off. "He tried to be a problem, so we killed him."

Rather a stark way to put it, but Oluchi supposed that anyone threatening Eha Dunham would probably deserve it, to see the greeting she had gotten on return.

"Will that cause us other problems?" Wolcott asked,

rather taken aback himself, if Oluchi was reading similarities in body language to what he had learned from Eha.

"It will not," Oluchi stepped up and bowed to the man. "I represent a plurality of the most important trade lords on Yisan, and they supported the operation. My principal looks forward to meeting you personally at some point, and discussing trade in earnest."

Wolcott studied him closer, like he was perhaps a rival.

Oluchi smiled that careful smile he gave to powerful men who might want to crush a competitor for a woman's affection, when they never realized that the women made those choices.

He supposed it made him seem less of a dominant personality, at least as men saw it, but usually it endeared him to the women. It was like listening to them want to bitch with a friendly smile on your face.

It did wonders here, as well. Wolcott's pupils narrowed, but then relaxed after a moment.

"Trade?" he asked in a voice that had at least a dozen layers of meaning shaded underneath.

"Absolutely, sir," Oluchi said with a nod. "At the very least, you represent a whole new culture, which will generate a demand for goods across Human space. I'm certain that my principal will want to help fulfill that demand. In turn, there will be Human goods in demand on your worlds. We are not formally part of the Rio Alliance, though we are loosely aligned. Trade is our centrality, rather than politics."

Oluchi did not miss the quick glance that flowed between the two Churquen and Lazarus. But he was expecting that. Best to have his motives on the table up front, especially if he wanted to get rich in the process of shaving off his percentages.

Wolcott turned to Grace next, studied her like another alien species. Considering how much darker her skin was from the three men, and the tight poof of curls, one could make that mistake, the first time dealing with Humans.

"And you?" Wolcott asked in a tone much more polite than the words themselves.

"Eduardo Martìnez, Oluchi's principal, tasked me with assisting Lazarus when it came time to use violence, and to protect him from repercussions," she said.

"So you did," Wolcott said dryly. "That time appears to have passed."

"I suspect Lazarus will continue to need help and protection," she smiled a sideways smile that both Churquen shared a moment later.

As inside jokes went, it wasn't that vague, but Oluchi could see how Lazarus might get into a variety of troubles and need friends. Looking around, that seemed to be the common theme with the group.

"Xiuying?" Wolcott turned to the last one.

"I'm just hired muscle along for the ride, mate," the man smiled ambiguously. "Also really useful when you need violence done."

"I've already got that covered," Wybert spoke up now in a tone Oluchi could only classify as aggrieved.

"Not the way you're holding that spear, buddy," Xiuying replied with just a hint of an edge to his voice. "Nobody ever taught you the proper way to grip it?"

"I am a warrior!" Wybert said, shuffling about a foot forward on all ten feet like a wave passing beneath him.

"I know a better grip you should use then," Xiuying held out an arm, like he expected Wybert to just hand him the spear. "May I?"

Oluchi wasn't the only one that suddenly held a breath. Wybert appeared to pout for a moment, and then blinked three of his eyes, which was really weird to watch, as the two on the outsides, almost like a horse or rabbit had, didn't blink at the same time.

Wybert pivoted and flipped the spear out, thankfully butt end first, rather than stabbing at Xiuying with it.

Lazarus had warned them about Wybert, but they'd all seen Xiuying in action.

"Right," Xiuying said, turning to the side and shifting so he was almost next to Wybert, rather than facing him. "Your fingers are all wrong, so you lose leverage. Useful to just punch someone with the butt end, but you almost never want to do that. Instead, hold it like this, see?"

Oluchi looked and realized that Wybert had been clutching the shaft in his whole fist. Xiuying was holding it more like a knife-fighter would, with thumb and middle finger controlling, and the other fingers just providing stability. Not that he'd ever had to use a knife that way.

That he would admit to.

"Edge wounds, understand?" Xiuying said slowly, carefully, deliberately. "Shaft stuns. Point kills. Always make sure every move you make is to keep them centered in front of you so you can stab at them with the killing tip. Front hand should only loosely hold, so you can adjust quickly. Here, you try."

Utter silence. Oluchi could have heard a key entering a lock three rooms away, as someone's husband got home unexpectedly.

Wybert reclaimed the spear and adjusted his fingers on it. Settled his weight some, all ten legs squatting with a quiet rumble.

The tip of the spear flickered out and back almost delicately. Oluchi wasn't all that versed in the sort of close combat Xiuying apparently did for a living. He was, after all, a lover, not a fighter. Still, he could see how much easier the spear moved.

"Thank you," Wybert said, grounding his spear and rotating his whole body around like a compass. The weird face might have smiled.

"We need to teach you some Yari, mate," Xiuying smiled. "Then you'll be all sorts of fun."

Oluchi wasn't sure he was prepared for that definition of fun, but he supposed that life was likely to be getting more dangerous, now that he had decided to change careers. At that point it would be useful to have expert killers around.

"Now what?" Oluchi asked the two commanders, mostly just to fully release the tension that had broken.

"Uniforms," Aileen suddenly announced.

"Uniforms, madam?" Oluchi turned to her and let the confusion show.

"I'm the Quartermaster on his ship," she smiled up at him. "As Lazarus said earlier, you'll need clothing, so we'll put you in Rio Alliance uniforms for now."

It dawned on Oluchi, looking at Addison Wolcott, that the man was wearing Rio colors, but the tan cotton tunic had been cut down to a simple vest, over which he was wearing a harness with pockets and loops. Both of the women had been dressed like civilians, Eha in a similar vest in blue and Aileen was in silvery capri pants and a vest in an off-white darker than cream but not down towards mustard.

"Will that cause a problem, boss?" Xiuying turned to Lazarus now.

"Not if you aren't wearing insignia or rank tabs, sailor," Lazarus said simply. "You three are civilians I rescued, or kidnapped, depending on how someone might interpret it, and I put you in appropriate clothing. Or rather, my Quartermaster did."

"I see," Oluchi said, somewhat crestfallen that he might have to dress like an office drone, rather than the dandy he'd been for a while.

"Alternatively," Lazarus smiled evilly at him, as if reading his mind, "I do have a tailor handy who can make Human clothing. We should have enough spare, if you prefer."

Oluchi nodded, unwilling to take the pretense too far. Grace shrugged, but she'd either look amazing in a burlap sack or vanish, depending on the needs of the situation.

He had an extremely good idea what that woman really did for Eduardo, regardless of whatever cover stories she might share.

"Whatever's easiest, mate," Xiuying said.

He'd worn tan before, so it might be like coming home for the man.

"This way," Aileen gestured for them to follow, so Oluchi took the lead.

He might as well figure out what his sartorial limits were now, and the capabilities of an alien tailor.

One adventure complete. New one tomorrow.

FORTY-ONE
ADDISON

ADDISON HAD WOUND himself around the coil in what had turned back into Lazarus's office, now that the man was back. Eha was coiled so close that their tails were tangled, as well as their hands. Ereshkiki Nisab was on Eha's far side, turned to watch them all with a different eye. The office was a little crowded.

That was good. He might have wanted to pace angrily and smash things, had there been room. He listened in a rage so deep that his tail hurt as he squeezed the chair.

"And then we lifted off and made rendezvous here," Lazarus finished off the tale.

Addison turned to Eha, studied her scales closely. He could see where a biped would show bruises, since they didn't have scales to cover them. Damage those Humans had done to his love.

Lazarus of Bethany had killed them all. And scorched the earth, if that was a term you could use when blowing up their ship and sinking it in an ocean for the fish to feed on.

And the man had been right about the office. Addison

needed to be seated, holding her hand. Otherwise, he might have exploded.

Addison took a deep breath and tried to loosen the kinks in his coils. He might have to go down to engineering and find a catwalk to hang from, if he really wanted to stretch things properly. It crossed his mind.

"Was it enough?" he asked Eha.

Her scales flared once as she drew a deep breath and considered his rage. Hers had been great, from the look in her eyes. Lazarus had used Human violence to extremes that Addison might have considered, had he been there.

"It was," Eha whispered a moment later.

Addison let some of his rage go. The Humans responsible were in a Human hell now, so there was nothing more he could do to them. Other Humans had volunteered to help.

Sure, they all had edges they were pursuing, but he supposed that this might be the biggest thing to happen to the Rio Alliance and all of Humanity since they first encountered the Atomarsk.

Up until recently, Addison had been a merchant director. He already understood that some people were going to get inordinately rich as a result of trading into and out of Innruld Space.

The Humans were just putting in the hard work now, to make sure that they got a place at the high table when that day came. If it had involved violence, Humans were exceptionally gifted at it.

And he would need Human violence to break the Innruld.

"So we trust the others?" Addison asked Lazarus.

"No," the man said, surprising him.

"No?"

"It could all have been an elaborate con job," Lazarus said. "Eduardo Martìnez might have set Strav Ardna up.

Oluchi Pryce might be a mole sent to get inside our organization, rather than a man with an eye to the main chance who's looking to get rich. Xiuying might be a sleeper agent of some sort, as he was a friend of Oluchi's who just happened to show up with a lot of firepower. Grave Savidge might be the most dangerous being I've ever met, and I used to do things like she and Xiuying did, when I was younger."

"You don't speak highly of the people who helped you rescue Eha?" Ereshkiki Nisab asked with three voices.

"Oh, I do," Lazarus replied. "But I don't know any of them that well. They might be what they seem, friends when I needed one. They might be a Trojan horse. I'm not planning on keying them into any systems, so let the crew know that these are civilians, not team mates, at least until we know better."

"You have a remarkable lack of faith in your own kind, Lazarus," Addison noted.

"Yes," he agreed. "I am still convinced that there is a spy at headquarters somewhere, feeding Westphalia information. That person nearly killed me. Strav Ardna nearly killed Eha. I think I've moved too fast for any useful conspiracy to accumulate around me, and I plan to continue doing that. As you've said, it is entirely possible that the Rio Alliance makes common cause with the Innruld to fight Westphalia, so they end up giving the overlords the sorts of technology that you would need to free yourselves."

"So things are only going to grow more complicated?" Eha spoke up.

"At least until we see which way people will jump," he nodded back. "I have a pretty good feeling about the three Humans I brought, or I would have left any of them behind on Yisan, but that's not the same as letting any of them have any power over me."

"Including Grace?" Eha asked in a tone Addison didn't understand.

"Especially Grace," Lazarus said.

Something cryptic passed between them. Addison wondered if she might tell him later. After he had finally calmed down.

"So now?" Addison asked as the silence stretched.

"Now, I've been awake too long," Lazarus said. "You'll put everyone to bed and lock the Humans out of any interesting places. Khyaa'sha can fix us all a meal in about ten hours, and then we'll start the run to Brasilia."

"The final confrontation?" Addison asked.

"Just the next one," Lazarus countered. "The final one takes place in Innruld Space."

Addison shivered in spite of how warm his rage had made him. The look on Lazarus's face promised a reckoning for the Innruld.

With or without Rio Alliance help.

FORTY-TWO

LAZARUS

LAZARUS WATCHED Addison and Eha slither down the corridor to their cabin in a harmony that was amazing to see. Addison seemed more relaxed, and Eha snuggling with him was the best distraction possible.

A sound caused him to look the other direction. Aileen was standing there, looking about as innocent as possible. Butter might not melt in her mouth right now.

"Dare I ask?" he smiled at her.

She shrugged, laughing only with her eyes.

"Lacking better direction, I showed the visitors that we had clothing and gear such as they might need to cover themselves for a few weeks while we sailed somewhere. Razors like you use for the men. Grace pointed out feminine products and explained what they did."

"Okay," Lazarus prompted her, waiting for the other shoe to drop.

"Since Eha's not using it, I went ahead and put everyone in the Ambassador's Suite aft," she smiled wickedly. "Grace, as it were, with two bodyguards, since Oluchi seems to want to keep a lower profile."

"Very good," Lazarus said, still waiting.

"Any other orders?" she asked politely.

"None, except that you might now also be considered my Boatswain," Lazarus said. "In addition to Quartermaster."

"So, what are you going to do with the Humans?" she asked, cocking her head finally and losing that grin.

He considered drawing her back into his office. But that sounded too formal. Instead, he started to walk forward, trailing the Churquen who had already vanished into a cabin. He and Aileen could talk in his cabin for now. A hand gestured for her to join in.

In his cabin, he settled in the chair and she climbed up onto the edge of the bed. The Ambassador space aft might be plush and roomy, but *Pancho* Oliveira had made his own quarters the same as all the officers got, which was the same volume as the enlisted, but he wasn't sharing space. It also let him keep things as compact as possible.

"What were you expecting me to do?" Lazarus asked Aileen as they stared at each other.

She paused, thrown off stride.

"Dunno," she finally admitted. "Maybe a happy-ever-after like Addison finally got with Eha?"

It was his turn to shrug.

"I've known her for less than two days," Lazarus said. "I don't think Oluchi represents a vast, underground conspiracy, only because I doubt anybody is that good, to pull something like that off at the drop of a hat. Or, if they are, I'm just glad they appear to be on our side."

"And Grace?" Aileen asked, rather bluntly, but she did that.

"Gorgeous, capable, intelligent, refined, dangerous," he cataloged her. "Oluchi had the luck and audacity to walk up and chat at that restaurant. But Eduardo Martìnez specifically selected her to be engaged with us. She works for him. I don't know what he's up to. Oluchi doesn't know, I don't think. I'm keyed up too much and maybe a little too paranoid, but I have my reasons."

"And a beautiful woman ready to throw herself at you gets your ruff up?" Aileen asked. "Who broke your heart?"

"That's a long story, and you'll probably have to get me drunk first, before I ever tell you the good parts."

"Oh, really?" she suddenly leaned forward. "You've never mentioned that bit, Lazarus."

He shrugged.

"I've been more or less married to the Navy for twenty years," he admitted. "Shore leave might involve a little tumble, but I've been inside secret bases and secured facilities for the last ten, so I wasn't in a position to talk to many women, except others in the same place."

"And it was one of those?" Aileen pressed.

"There have been a few," he replied. "Nothing serious, mind you. None worth marrying."

"And Grace Savidge?"

"Frighteningly perfect, Aileen Enjehn," Lazarus smiled. "If anything, I'm afraid of getting my head turned, to use the ancient saying."

"Why would that be a bad thing, Lazarus of Bethany?" she smiled back.

He felt the seriousness drop down on him like a net.

"*Ajax* was a secret project to build a weapon capable of defeating Westphalia," he said, sobering. "Someone put me in a trap and nearly killed me. I intended to fly into a star with *Ajax*, so they never found out the truth. Instead, I blundered into Innruld Space and found you and the gang. I have a responsibility to you and Addison, since I didn't take *Ajax* and go break the Innruld directly. We'll need the Rio Alliance, but I don't know who to trust, outside of *Shiva Zephyr Glaive*. That includes three new Humans, one of whom might have been sent by Central Casting to seduce me. Might all be a coincidence, but I'm running on really long odds, and about to sail right back to Brasilia."

"Out of the frying pan, and into the fire?" she asked, also sober now.

He nodded.

"What can I do?" she asked.

"Keep being you," Lazarus decided. "Competent, friendly, sharp. Maybe the newcomers work out. Maybe it's all a trap. I just don't know."

"You've got us," she nodded.

"You and Addison are the reason I'm still alive, Aileen," Lazarus reminded her. "If I thought I could break the Innruld myself, I'd recruit us a Human crew out here, but I'm afraid they'd all be pirates of some sort, or moles sent to steal the ship."

"Is *Ajax* really that dangerous?" she asked.

"Yes, it is," Lazarus said. "I designed it to win a war. Turns out that might just be the first one I have to win."

She nodded, finally understanding from the look on her face.

Their species really didn't understand violence on the sorts of scales that Humans practiced.

But Lazarus of Bethany had already decided he would do whatever it took to free his friends, and all their kin, from the Innruld.

With, or without the Rio Alliance.

READ MORE

Be sure to read all the books in the Lazarus Alliance series!

Escape
Return
Rebellion
Revolution
Liberation
Retribution
Alliance

Available at your favorite retailers!

ABOUT THE AUTHOR

Blaze Ward writes science fiction in the Alexandria Station universe (Jessica Keller, The Science Officer, The Story Road, etc.) as well as several other science fiction universes, such as Star Dragon, the Dominion, and more. He also writes odd bits of high fantasy with swords and orcs. In addition, he is the Editor and Publisher of *Boundary Shock Quarterly Magazine*. You can find out more at his website www.blazeward.com, as well as Facebook, Goodreads, and other places.

Blaze's works are available as ebooks, paper, and audio, and can be found at a variety of online vendors. His newsletter comes out regularly, and you can also follow his blog on his website. He really enjoys interacting with fans, and looks forward to any and all questions—even ones about his books!

Never miss a release!
If you'd like to be notified of new releases, sign up for my newsletter.

http://www.blazeward.com/newsletter/

Buy More!
Did you know that you can buy directly from my website?

https://www.blazeward.com/shop/

Connect with Blaze!

Web: www.blazeward.com
Boundary Shock Quarterly (BSQ):
https://www.boundaryshockquarterly.com/

ABOUT KNOTTED ROAD PRESS

Knotted Road Press fiction specializes in dynamic writing set in mysterious, exotic locations.

Knotted Road Press non–fiction publishes autobiographies, business books, cookbooks, and how–to books with unique voices.

Knotted Road Press creates DRM–free ebooks as well as high–quality print books for readers around the world.

With authors in a variety of genres including literary, poetry, mystery, fantasy, and science fiction, Knotted Road Press has something for everyone.

Knotted Road Press
www.KnottedRoadPress.com